George Moore

The Strike at Arlingford

Play in Three Acts

George Moore

The Strike at Arlingford
Play in Three Acts

ISBN/EAN: 9783337401375

Printed in Europe, USA, Canada, Australia, Japan

Cover: Foto ©Andreas Hilbeck / pixelio.de

More available books at **www.hansebooks.com**

THE STRIKE AT ARLINGFORD.

THE STRIKE AT ARLINGFORD

PLAY IN THREE ACTS

By GEORGE MOORE

LONDON
WALTER SCOTT, LIMITED
24 WARWICK LANE
1893

NOTE.

In my own conception of my play the labour dispute is an externality to which I attach little importance. What I applied myself to in the composition of " The Strike at Arlingford" was the development of a moral idea. I leave the play itself to explain this idea.

G. M.

CHARACTERS.

JOHN REID.

BARON STEINBACH.

FRED HAMER.

LADY ANNE TRAVERS.

ELLEN SANDS.

FOX,
SIMON, } *Miners.*

FOOTMAN.

MINERS.

THE STRIKE AT ARLINGFORD.

ACT I.

SCENE. — *Drawing-room at* LADY ANNE TRAVERS'. *Bow window opening on lawn at back right. Door back, window left, door right. Writing-table, couch, arm-chairs, rich furniture. When the curtain rises the door at back, middle of stage, is opened by the* FOOTMAN.

Mr. HAMER *is shown in.*

FOOTMAN.

I will give her ladyship your card.

(*The door is closed.* HAMER *looks round, and having assured himself that he is not observed, opens a note-book and begins taking notes of the contents of the room.* BARON STEINBACH *appears at window*

opening on to lawn.   After watching
HAMER *a moment he enters ;* HAMER
turns to him with some slight embarrass-
ment.)

HAMER.

I come from the *Durham Mercury*. Here is
my card.

STEINBACH (*reads*).

" Mr. Fred Hamer, representative of the
Durham Mercury." (*Speaks*) You want to see
Lady Anne ?

HAMER.

I should like to.   I've come from Durham for
the purpose of writing some descriptive articles
on the state of the town during the strike of
colliers. I hope that Lady Anne will be kind
enough to grant me an interview.

STEINBACH.

In any case you intend a descriptive article
on her drawing-room.

HAMER.

I'm afraid you caught me in the act—just a
memorandum of the room. This is her drawing-
room, the room she lives in, I suppose ?

(HAMER *looks at* STEINBACH, *wondering who he is.* STEINBACH *speaks with lofty superiority, and yet without vulgarity.*)

STEINBACH.

This is Lady Anne's drawing-room. But I do not think that she will be able to grant you an interview. Lady Anne, you see, has only just returned from abroad. She has a great deal of business to attend to, and I hardly think that the present time is a convenient one. She has not yet got over the fatigue of the journey.

HAMER.

She has been, I believe, about a week in Arlingford ?

STEINBACH (*looking at him sharply, and answering sharply*).

Yes, about a week.

HAMER.

I presume that these labour troubles had something to do with her ladyship's sudden return ?

STEINBACH.

I am afraid I cannot answer you. However,

I may tell you that it is not likely that Lady
Anne will be able to spare the time for an interview this morning. I have come to speak to
her on business. I tell you this, for I know that
you newspaper people are very hard worked,
and that your time is not your own.

HAMER.

Thank you. But—I have sent in my card,
stating my business, and if Lady Anne is as
busy as you say, she will probably make an
appointment. I am in no hurry.

(*Sits down and takes up book. Annoyed, the*
BARON *walks towards the window; he
turns, and seeing that* HAMER *does not
intend to leave, he crosses left, stops, reads
the card, pauses, and then speaks.*)

STEINBACH.

I see you come from Durham, Mr. Hamer.
(HAMER *lays down the book, and looks up quite
pleased at the interruption.*) How are things in
your neighbourhood? Any signs of fresh labour
troubles?

HAMER.

The miners are, I think, waiting to see how
things will turn out in Arlingford.

STEINBACH.

Very likely; and if the battle is lost here, we may expect strikes all over the North of England.

(HAMER *looks at him curiously, wondering who is this grand and somewhat authoritative individual.*)

Wattsbury ought to have taught trades unionism a lesson; it received a severe defeat there.

HAMER.

It did indeed. But the men would have won all along the line if it had not been for the energy and decision of Baron Steinbach. He is the most determined foe that trades unionism has. He sees that the concessions which the men ask in the name of Justice are stepping-stones to the utter destruction of capital.

STEINBACH.

Don't you think he is right?

HAMER.

Unquestionably, from his point of view.

STEINBACH (*in a more conciliatory tone*).

Were you at Wattsbury?

HAMER.

Yes, I interviewed the strike leaders and as
many of the directors as I could. I was most
anxious to get an interview with Baron Steinbach, but he was always engaged. An interview
with him would have been most interesting.
He is a man of ideas, and could express his
views regarding the necessity of capital.

STEINBACH (*laughing*).

Your flattering remarks make it impossible
for me to leave you any longer in doubt as
to whom you are talking to — I am Baron
Steinbach.

HAMER (*jumping up and somewhat overcome*).

Oh, indeed, I am sure I had no idea—I am
pleased to have had the honour of meeting you.

STEINBACH (*bows*).

I read your interviews, and must confess that
they were singularly free from prejudice. You
have the talent of conveying an interesting and
truthful reflection of life.

HAMER (*delighted*).

I am glad you liked my articles. I was

just saying that I tried to get an interview with you during the Wattsbury strike, but you were always engaged.

STEINBACH.

Did it occur to you that perhaps I did not want to be interviewed?

HAMER (*laughing*).

Perhaps it did. But are you sure you're not mistaken? The strike leaders are always anxious to express their views.

STEINBACH.

The position of the socialist leaders and the capitalists regarding publicity is quite different. They have everything, we have nothing to gain by the publication of our views. In my opinion the battle on our side should be conducted in silence.

(*Perceiving that* HAMER *is listening intently he stops short.*)

But I see that you are interviewing me.

HAMER.

I wish you would develop that idea. You

were saying that the battle on your side should be conducted in silence.

STEINBACH.

If I were to develop that idea I should be acting contrary to the principles I profess.

HAMER.

But while we are waiting for Lady Anne it would be most interesting if——

STEINBACH (*laughing*).

I see you are a born journalist—the effective article is your principle.

HAMER.

My principle and my interest.

STEINBACH (*laughing*).

Even if I wished to express my views I'm afraid this is no time to do so. I have come to Arlingford to see my friend Lady Anne Travers.

HAMER.

I hope you have come with some project of settlement. But you are against all com-promise; you would force the miners to accede to your terms. But perhaps Lady Anne may incline towards the principle that labour disputes should be settled by arbitration.

STEINBACH.

If ever I desire to express my views on capital and labour I shall be glad to entrust their transmission to your intelligence; in the meantime, do not try to interview me against my will.

HAMER.

You will excuse my hoping that Lady Anne will see no harm——

STEINBACH.

I think that all expressions of opinion at the present moment would be injudicious.

HAMER.

I will not presume to argue that point with you, Baron Steinbach. But may I ask you if you think that Lady Anne will keep us waiting much longer?

STEINBACH.

I have already told you, Mr. Hamer, that

2

I believe Lady Anne is still suffering from the fatigues of her journey—that I have come to talk with her on important business.

HAMER.

If I were in your house, Baron Steinbach, I should at once retire, but as I am in Lady Anne Travers's, perhaps you will excuse me if I wait until Lady Anne herself decides if she can see me.

(*The door on the right opens and* LADY ANNE *enters.*)

LADY ANNE.

Oh, how do you do, my dear Baron? How good of you to come! Who is——

HAMER.

I come from the *Durham Mercury.* You have my card in your hand, Lady Anne.

STEINBACH.

I have told Mr. Hamer that I do not think it is advisable that you should express any opinion regarding the strike.

LADY ANNE.

You see, Mr. Hamer, I only arrived a few
days ago from abroad. I have been little in
Arlingford since my husband's death ; besides,
I have exceedingly important business to discuss with Baron Steinbach. You must excuse
me.

HAMER.

I was about to explain to Baron Steinbach
when you entered that the object of this visit
was not merely to interview you regarding the
strike—I easily divine what your views are—
but to ask you if I may be present at one
o'clock, when you receive the deputation.

STEINBACH (*to* LADY ANNE).

Have you consented to receive another deputation ?

LADY ANNE.

I could hardly refuse. Do you think I was
wrong ?

STEINBACH.

I don't think much good will come of re-open-
ing the question. You intend to stand by your
first offer and to grant nothing further ?

LADY ANNE.

I can make no further concession, that is certain. But I do not think it would look well to refuse to receive the deputation.

STEINBACH.

Perhaps not.

HAMER.

The account I shall furnish will be impartial; you know that, Baron Steinbach. But should you refuse to allow me to report the proceedings, John Reid or his *fiancée*, Ellen Sands, will send in a report, and you know what a one-sided version that will be.

STEINBACH (*stops to think*).

Yes, it is as you say; I prefer your report to theirs, and I have no objection to offer. Lady Anne, will you allow Mr. Hamer to accompany the deputation ?

LADY ANNE.

I shall be very glad if you will consent to be present.

HAMER.

Thank you. At once o'clock, then. You have

just come back from the south, Lady Anne?
This is the room you live in. That cabinet
is Chippendale?

LADY ANNE.

No, old Italian.

HAMER.

I should like to have the impressions gathered
on your journey, but when you are less busy.
Your drawing-room looks on a garden. You
are fond of gardening, I suppose? One of
these days, before you leave, Lady Anne, you
will favour me, I hope, with your views and your
impressions; and, perhaps, Baron Steinbach, I
shall be able to persuade you to favour me with
your views regarding the necessity of capital?
Most interesting, I'm sure.

STEINBACH.

We'll talk about that later on.

HAMER.

I hope so.

(*Exit.*)

(BARON STEINBACH *returns from the door.*
LADY ANNE *advances to meet him, her
hand extended.*)

STEINBACH.

It is such a pleasure to see you again, Anne.

LADY ANNE (*with an almost imperceptible moving away from him*).

And I am so glad to see you. I wrote to you, because I believe you to be my friend.

STEINBACH.

You have no better friend. When I received your letter, I called for the Bradshaw, and I told my servant to pack my portmanteau at once. Then I threw myself into an arm-chair and read your letter over and over again.

LADY ANNE.

There was not much to read.

STEINBACH.

No; your letters are always the same curt little epistles. . . . A little statement in a fine, delicate handwriting. (*Taking her hand.*) Your hand is your handwriting—that decisive little writing with its very distinctive slope. (*She withdraws her hand.*) It was a great pleasure to receive your letter, and in the train I watched the hedge-rows, thinking that with every one I was some yards nearer to you.

LADY ANNE.

It was very good of you. You are very good to me. I want you to be my friend.

STEINBACH.

If I were not your friend, do you think that I would have left important business and come to you at an hour's notice? I didn't wait for the express. I came by the slow train, because it arrived here ten minutes sooner.

LADY ANNE.

You've arrived none too soon. Things are in a frightful way here. I don't know what will become of me! What would you advise?

STEINBACH.

We've all the afternoon to talk business. I want to tell you that I think you as charming as ever.

LADY ANNE.

If you wouldn't make love to me.

STEINBACH.

Have I not a right?

LADY ANNE.

I'd sooner have you as a friend.

STEINBACH.

You didn't always think like that, Anne.

LADY ANNE.

I always told you that I was a cold woman, and I'm in too great trouble now to think about love. (STEINBACH *looks at her doubtfully.*) I know you don't believe me; men never will believe. (*A pause.*)

STEINBACH.

I never could make out whether you liked me, or what you intended.

LADY ANNE.

I always liked you, my dear Baron, but——

STEINBACH.

My dear Anne, let us be frank with one another; you've treated me very badly.

LADY ANNE.

Have I?

STEINBACH.

Think of it. We met at a dinner-party about two years ago, and it has been going on ever since.

LADY ANNE.

You took me down to dinner.

STEINBACH.

And we were friends before we got to the dining-room; and next day you wrote asking me to lunch, and you began your letter " My dear Baron."

LADY ANNE.

I didn't mean anything by that. I told you in the drawing-room that very night that you were mistaken in me.

STEINBACH.

It wasn't so much that I was mistaken as that I was unlucky. It was not to be; I felt from the first I was not going to be your lover. One always knows.

LADY ANNE.

How strange men are! Is that what a man thinks when he is introduced to a woman—am I or am I not going to be her lover?

STEINBACH.

Only when one is in love. I thought you the most fascinating woman I had seen for a long time. You seemed to like me, yet I only once thought that my instinct had deceived me.

LADY ANNE.

When was that?

STEINBACH.

The first time I lunched alone with you. I was standing on the hearth-rug smoking a cigarette, thinking how I should tell you that I loved you. You must have guessed my embarrassment, for you got up and walked so close to me that I quite naturally took you in my arms.

LADY ANNE.

It was then that you thought that you were mistaken.

STEINBACH.

Yes, and the mistake was pardonable, for with your head lying on my shoulder, you told me you were going out of town, and it was arranged that I was to meet you.

LADY ANNE.

What could I do? My friends wrote to say they were going to send for me to the station.

STEINBACH.

You put me off till the summer, till you went abroad to take the waters at Carlsbad or Contrexville, I forget which. The day was arranged for your departure, but I knew that something would happen to prevent it, and something did happen.

LADY ANNE.

It was not my fault. You know it wasn't.

STEINBACH.

Apparently not. You told me the whole circumstances three months after.

LADY ANNE.

I could not have acted otherwise than I did. But when I asked you to come to the Riviera you couldn't leave London. That was not my fault!

STEINBACH.

Nor mine; it was the moment of the Baring crisis, and for a fortnight I did not know that I should have a thousand left to go on with. When I wrote to you later on, you sent a telegram telling me not to come.

LADY ANNE.

I had friends staying with me. There always did seem to be some hitch. And now I am like you were in the Baring crisis; in a week's time I may not have a thousand pounds to my name. How can you expect me to think of love at such a time? (*Rises and crosses.*)

STEINBACH.

Tell me exactly what your position is.

LADY ANNE.

I cannot go into details.

STEINBACH.

I don't want the details. I'll get them from the books; just the main facts. (*Lights a cigarette.*)

LADY ANNE.

As far as I understand, the dispute resolves itself to this: The men want a rise of twenty per cent. all round. There are other demands, the abolition of what they ·call "Billy Fairplay." It has something to do with getting rid of the refuse.

STEINBACH.

I know. Have the men had an increase before?

LADY ANNE.

Yes; last year a increase of five per cent. was demanded on account of an anticipated advance in the price of coal.

STEINBACH.

You conceded the rise in wages and the advance in coal did not come off?

LADY ANNE.

Exactly.

STEINBACH.

So the money in the mine, out of which you all get your living, is five per cent. poorer than last year?

LADY ANNE.

I suppose so. (*Sits R. table.*) They contribute nothing towards the working expenses, and now they want another rise of twenty per cent. If the mine belonged to the miners, it could not be worked on such a scale of wages.

STEINBACH (*walking to and fro*).

I should think not indeed. It is impossible to work a mine on the co-operative principle. At the end of six months they would have to reduce the scale of wages; in a year they would be in bankruptcy, and the mine in ruins.

LADY ANNE.

My manager tells me that we could not grant this twenty per cent. and work the mine at a profit. Even if it were possible, nothing would be left for me.   I cannot afford to grant more than five per cent.

STEINBACH.

I would not have you raise their wages one per cent., nor grant any concession whatsoever. Admit the principle of concession, and bit by bit they will wring our property from us.   Our interests are common, and if we were half as united in our actions as these fellows we should very soon trample out the labour movement. (*Sits.*)   When did the men leave work?

LADY ANNE.

Three weeks ago.

STEINBACH.

Do you think they are well supplied with funds?

LADY ANNE.

I think not.   A week ago they would have accepted our terms.

STEINBACH.

A mistake, a fatal mistake, to offer any terms.

If *I* had my way, the declaration of every strike should be accompanied with a declaration of a reduction of wages. They accept our terms, or we lose the battle sooner or later.

LADY ANNE.

It is easy for you to speak like that; your capital is unlimited, mine is not, and if the pumps were to be stopped, and the water got the upper hand, the mine might never be got back into working order.

STEINBACH.

There is always non-unionist labour to be had if you offer the price.

LADY ANNE.

They say that there is hardly any non-unionist labour; besides, my resources are limited.

STEINBACH.

The other mine-owners should help you.

LADY ANNE.

They are afraid the strike will spread.

STEINBACH.

Personal selfishness will prove our ruin in the end. That's the weak point in our armour. And you tell me they refused your offer of five per cent. Why was that?

LADY ANNE.

The great labour leader, John Reid, came down here to conduct the strike, and it was owing to his influence that the men resolved to accept no abatement on their original demands.

STEINBACH.

I know him; we met at Wattsbury. He is a poet as well as a socialist leader; a curious combination, socialism and poetry. I see no connection between hob-nails and sonnets, bull-pups and——

LADY ANNE (*rises*).

His poems are not in the least like that. Here is his last volume. (*Takes book from table.*) *Nostalgia;* charming title, isn't it? and there are charming things in it.

STEINBACH.

It is strange that, notwithstanding all your

trouble, you should be able to find time to interest
yourself in poetry.   This taste in poetry is quite
new in you.   (LADY ANNE *continues reading.*
STEINBACH *watches.*)   One would think you
were personally interested in the author.

LADY ANNE (*laying the book down*).

I'm afraid that that is just it.   You see, we
are old friends.

STEINBACH.

What *do* you mean, Anne?

LADY ANNE.

Yes, old friends, though we have not seen
each other for ten years.   Ten years ago he
was my father's secretary—he was eighteen and
I was seventeen.

STEINBACH.

Oh, I see, a boy and girl flirtation.

LADY ANNE.

Yes, I suppose it was that.   We used to
stand on the terrace and look at the sun setting.
He wrote verses which he used to send me.   It

was a pretty romance while it lasted. (*Sits on sofa.*)

STEINBACH.

And how was it broken off?

LADY ANNE.

When I was eighteen. I understood that I could not marry my father's secretary.

STEINBACH.

And John Reid was dismissed, and he told you that you had broken his heart.

LADY ANNE.

John Reid was not Lord Elwin's servant. He was just as much a gentleman as my father.

STEINBACH.

Ah! that explains a good deal in John Reid. He used to puzzle me; I could see that his plebeian airs were more or less an affectation. I understand it all now.

LADY ANNE.

And do you think better of him?

STEINBACH.

No, indeed.   I should have liked him better as a working-man fighting the battle of his class. So he is a mere parcel of renunciations, a frantic egotism——

LADY ANNE.

Egotism!   But he surrenders all things for an idea.

STEINBACH.

Renunciations are often but the efforts of the feeble to realise themselves.   So he is no more than a convert.   I have little taste for conversions of any kind.   You know, my dear Anne——

LADY ANNE.

I believe it is disagreeable to you that any one should even try to be good.

STEINBACH.

Ah! trying to be good!   But I see that you

can only think of your old lover. Tell me about
him. He said that you had broken his heart.

LADY ANNE.

He did say that his heart was broken.

STEINBACH.

And in the following year you married Sir
Francis Travers. Five years ago he died
leaving you a rich widow, and your old lover
heads a strike of your miners, little thinking
that Lady Anne Travers is the Anne that he
loved. You were a lovely girl ; how much you
must have meant to him !

LADY ANNE.

Yes, he did love me, perhaps as no one else
ever did.

STEINBACH.

A most romantic situation ; and the young
man comes here suspecting nothing ?

LADY ANNE.

He suspected nothing the day before yesterday.

STEINBACH.

Then you have written to him?

LADY ANNE.

No; I went to see him.

STEINBACH.

Where? At his lodgings?

LADY ANNE.

No. At the committee rooms.

STEINBACH.

And you saw him?

LADY ANNE.

No, I didn't see him. He was not there.

STEINBACH.

But you do not care for him?

LADY ANNE.

Care for him?   No; but I should like to see
him again.

STEINBACH.

So that, through his influence, you might
settle this dispute to your advantage?

LADY ANNE.

That is all.   (*Rises.*)

STEINBACH.

Did you meet any one at the committee
rooms?

LADY ANNE.

Yes; his sweetheart, Ellen Sands.   They are
engaged to be married.   I can't congratu-
late him on his choice—a most unformed
young person.   I have heard since that she is
a school-mistress turned socialist; the girl who
believes she has a mission, and would hang on
to a man for its accomplishment.

STEINBACH.

I know the type. The feeble who are in earnest.

LADY ANNE.

I cannot think what he sees in her.

STEINBACH.

Did you leave any message for him?

LADY ANNE.

I wrote a note, but fearing she might see it, I tore it up, and left some flowers I had with me.

STEINBACH.

How like a woman! You knew that leaving the flowers would cause Ellen Sands extreme annoyance.

LADY ANNE.

I did not care whether I annoyed her. It was a bunch of heliotrope, and he always associated that perfume with me. He will think and think. She will describe me over and over again, and then suddenly he will remember. I don't think I have changed very much.

STEINBACH.

It is a pity in a way, for if he knew nothing at all about it, what would his consternation not have been on finding himself face to face with you!

LADY ANNE.

I daresay he will be sufficiently troubled as it is.

STEINBACH.

You forget that rejected love turns to hate.

LADY ANNE.

Do you mean that you are going to hate me? You know, Edward, that it was not my fault. Something went wrong from the first; as you said, we weren't lucky. Why cannot you be my friend? (*Sits.*)

STEINBACH.

I'm too much a man of the world to quarrel with a woman because she won't love me. But I understand the whole matter now. When you found that the strike leader was your old lover, you went straight to him, but finding him engaged to be married, you telegraphed to me. Most womanly and most modern.

LADY ANNE (*rises*).

How horrible and cynical you are : you like to misinterpret. I wrote to you because I thought you were my friend.

STEINBACH.

Don't let us talk any more about friendship— you make the world odious to me. There are two reasons why I should help you. First, because you are a pretty woman ; second, be- cause it is my interest to defeat these socialists whenever I can ; on triumphing over you they triumph over me. If you consent to put your affair entirely in my hands, I will do the best I can for you.

LADY ANNE.

Will you? And will you stop and receive this deputation?

STEINBACH.

On conditions that you do not concede any- thing above your first offer of five per cent.

LADY ANNE.

Very well; and now let us talk of other things. What have you been doing all this long while? Who have you been making love to?

STEINBACH.

To no one.   You're the only woman who interests me.   (*Enter* FOOTMAN.)

FOOTMAN.

The deputation is waiting, my lady.

LADY ANNE (*to* BARON STEINBACH).
Shall we receive it here?

STEINBACH.

Why not?

LADY ANNE.

Show them up.   (*Exit* FOOTMAN.)   Do you think you'll be able to get them to accept my offer?

STEINBACH.

I think so.   These strike leaders are beginning to feel afraid of me.

FOOTMAN.

The deputation, my lady.

(*Enter* JOHN REID, HAMER, ELLEN SANDS, *and six Miners. The Miners are impressed by their surroundings.* LADY ANNE *signs to the deputation to sit ; some do, some do not.* STEINBACH *accosts the men.*)

STEINBACH.

So you're out on strike, it appears. (ELLEN *advances.* STEINBACH *interrupts her.*) Well, I shall be pleased to talk over things with you. (*Rolls up his chair, and settles himself comfortably.*) Well, what have you to say to me ?

ELLEN SANDS.

It is with Lady Anne Travers——

STEINBACH.

Lady Anne has placed her business in my hands.

ELLEN.

There is no reason whatever, then——

STEINBACH.

Oh yes, there is. We have met before, Miss Sands—in the Wattsbury strike, which ended so disastrously for the men. You did not expect to see me here. (*Turning from* ELLEN *to the men.*) Now, you look like quiet, industrious fellows. I daresay you were pulled out against your will; you had nothing to do with getting up this strike, and would have been glad to have accepted Lady Anne's handsome offer of five per cent.?

ELLEN.

If you think that you are mistaken. It is not the idle and indifferent, it is the real workman that rises against you, and says, " Since you condemn me to starvation, I prefer to be at liberty, and not to die of hunger whilst I am filling your pockets."

STEINBACH.

This is personal animosity, the result of your defeat at Wattsbury. I am not of opinion that these men should suffer to gratify your vanity.

ELLEN.

We have not come here to listen to your jibes.   John, won't you speak?

REID.

Perhaps, Ellen ; but from the tone that Baron Steinbach is taking, I doubt if it is worth our while to enter into discussion with him.

ELLEN.

That is my opinion.   I never saw any good come of discussion.   We are strong enough in Arlingford to dictate our own terms.

STEINBACH.

You were of the same opinion at Wattsbury. However, as the men are here, they shall have the facts of the case—they shall know what they are doing.   If they then please to sacrifice themselves, they can.   You would like to know the facts?

FOX.

Yes, yes ; let's 'ear what e's to say.

STEINBACH.

Now, men, I have gone into the calculation, and am prepared to prove what I say, step by step, to any one you may select. At present I will merely state the results. You have had recently a rise of five per cent. in wages, which was conceded to you as a rise in prices was anticipated. The rise in prices did not come, and in consequence that rise in wages simply diminished the value of the mine, the property from whose success comes your only chance of livelihood. And in these circumstances you demand a further increase in the rate of wages to the extent of twenty per cent.; that, if granted, would again diminish the value of the mine to less than nothing. To work it under such conditions would cost five thousand a year more than it would pay. I can give you the figures for it.

ELLEN.

We know that argument, and dispute it no more. We say :—You have convinced us beyond the shadow of a doubt that you cannot give us twenty per cent. We say we don't doubt your word; we say we don't doubt your figures; and then we say, nevertheless, we want our twenty per cent., and somehow the capitalists manage in the end to concede it.

STEINBACH.

This is mere violence. I appeal to you men that if your leaders' demand was granted the mine would have to be worked at a loss of five thousand a year for your benefit, and I ask you if you think it likely that we shall do this?

MINERS.

Not likely, not likely.

(REID *steps forward as if to speak.* LADY ANNE *rises.*)

LADY ANNE.

Excuse me a moment. I should like to say a word. Three generations ago no one dreamed there was coal here. The land was waste. My husband's grandfather was a great mineralogist; he found in the soil the signs that told his practised eye that coal lay hidden far beneath it. He had saved a little money by the hard labour of half a lifetime, and with that—all he had—

he bought the land we stand on. . . . His son, and subsequently my husband, devoted their lives to the mine, and by dint of patience, courage, and self-denial they forced it at length to yield a profit. You did not do this; it was not your brains;—it was not your money that created this property.

ELLEN.

The sophistries of all capitalists; there is nothing of value in the world save the labour of man.

LADY ANNE.

And now to matters that concern you as much as they concern me, for our fortunes are inextricably bound together. Remember, before you decide, that the thing once done cannot be undone. If the furnaces are once stopped, I am ruined, and so are you. The mine will be closed, and your chance of changing your minds will be gone then. In place of some fancied benefit, you will have brought this upon yourselves, that you, your wives and children, will have to go among strangers and beg of them for

4

that work that you will have made it impossible for me to give you here. (*Goes up to Miners.*)

A MINER.

I say, boys, what do you think of it?

ELLEN.

Steady, men.   Take time.

FOX.

I'd be main sorry to see the mine closed.   I've worked there from a lad—my father and uncle was killed in it.

SIMON.

Say, master, what about Billy Fairplay? Will you say the dross shall be paid for?

STEINBACH.

Our offer is the same as before.   Five per cent. rise, or if you like better, three per cent. rise and twopence a ton for the dross.

FOX.

That's good enough for us ; what do ye say, lads?

(*Applause, and murmurs of acquiescence among the Miners.*)

ELLEN.

John, John! (*They come down together.*) They are all falling away from us. Speak as you did the other day in the market-place.

REID.

I never approved of this deputation, Ellen. Such a question as this is not to be discussed in Lady Anne's drawing-room.

ELLEN.

There's no better place. (*She turns to the Miners.*) It is here they should tell her the story of their wrongs; of the despair of their wives, of the hungry complaining of their little ones. It is here that they should ask her if she wishes to destroy them utterly.

> (LADY ANNE *has been talking to the Miners,
> who are overcome by her condescension;
> she listens with a look of contempt to*
> ELLEN'S *speech.*)

There is a word to be said, and if you speak it you'll be listened to.

REID (*with the air of a man who has come
to a sudden decision*).

Lady Anne, I must remind you that a
deputation can only be addressed through its
responsible spokesman.

LADY ANNE.

Do you dictate to me my behaviour in my
own house?

REID.

No; but I am responsible for these men. (*He
pushes back the men to whom* LADY ANNE *has
been speaking.*) I speak for them; and I say
that though they are overwhelmed by your
consideration in noticing their existence after
years of neglect, that though for the moment
they are confused by the laws of arithmetic,
yet they are not cowards, but men. They come
out of your mine because their burden was too
heavy to be borne! They will not take it on
their shoulders again unless you can lighten it.

LADY ANNE.

But it is my wish to do so. I was telling

them that their property and mine were linked together.

REID.

Words without meaning. (*Murmurs.*) We have a distinct demand; do you grant that?

LADY ANNE.

It is unreasonable.   It would ruin me.

REID.

So it has been said.   Then this concession of five per cent. is the only one?

STEINBACH.

Five per cent., or three per cent. and twopence for the refuse.

REID.

We cannot accept that.

A MINER.

Why not?

ELLEN.

Mr. Reid will tell you.   John, speak as you

did the other day! Explain—tell them how this lady's wealth is the result of their labour.

REID.

You want to know why you should refuse her ladyship's offer. Because you've taken it into your heads that you intend to live like men and not like beasts. But you're told that if you do not live like beasts, that this lady will be ruined. Look round you, mates; this is a nice place to be ruined in. Never were you in such a place before; feast your eyes upon it, and feel the tread of the carpet under your feet, and breathe the soft scented air. All your homes taken together would not suffice to purchase this room. And the rings on the fingers of that delicate lady are worth more than you can earn in a year of labour. Look at Baron Steinbach and look at yourselves! Look at her, and think of your sisters and wives! She has told you what her husband, her husband's father, and her husband's grandfather did for the mine; but she has not said a word about what your fathers and your grandfathers did for it. From her ancestors she inherited the right to live in idleness, but yours could only bequeath

to you the right to labour for her benefit.
You've taken up arms against this injustice ;
you're fighting not only for yourselves, but for
your wives and children.   You're fighting to
give them decent meals and decent homes, and
when we've led you within sight of victory, you
hesitate . . . Have you brought me here to tell
her that you'd starve like brutes rather than
she should want for anything ?   I want to know.
Now which is it going to be ?

FOX.

Say, Master John, but thee do speak fine ;
let's 'ave a word about the strike fund.   We
cannot see the bairns starve afore our eyes.

REID.

This morning's post brought us help and
promise of help.   The money is all right.

SIMON.

If Mr. Reid says the money is right, I'm for
the strike.

REID.

Will you hold out now, lads ?

A MINER.

Of course we will ; give us yer 'and.

ANOTHER MINER.

Hurrah, boys !

MINERS.

Never fear, sir ; we'll hold out.   Hurrah for
the strike, boys !   (*Cheers.*)

(*Exeunt Miners.*)

LADY ANNE.

This is disgraceful.   (*To* ELLEN.)   Will you
persuade your friend to make a bear-garden of
some other place than my drawing-room ?

ELLEN.

The men have done no harm to your drawing-
room ; a few cheers won't hurt your furniture.

STEINBACH.

Then the strike is to go on at all costs.

ELLEN.

Certainly.   Come, John, you've done excellently well ; come.

REID.

I will follow you in a moment. I have a word to say to Baron Steinbach.

(*Exit* ELLEN.)

STEINBACH.

You are mistaken, Mr. Reid. I have nothing to say to you.

REID.

Is Lady Anne determined that this battle should be fought out to the end? (*Catching* LADY ANNE'S *eye*.) I am sorry if the violence of my words has prejudiced you against the men; I was never in favour of the deputation.

LADY ANNE.

You mistook my drawing-room for a tavern. (*Pauses.*) Your manner was once more courteous. Have you forgotten? Perhaps you do not know——

REID.

I have not forgotten. I wish you to understand that personal motives do not count with me in this matter; circumstances forced me to

go further than I intended; but when I meet
my comrades in council, your interest shall not
unduly suffer.

> (HAMER *comes down the stage and advances
> towards* STEINBACH, *who is standing
> near* LADY ANNE.)

HAMER.

Excuse me, Baron Steinbach. You could not
state your case to ignorant men. Now the
advantage of the press is——

LADY ANNE (*eagerly*).

I should not like any incorrect statement to
get into the papers, Baron; you will oblige me
if you give Mr. Hamer all necessary information.

> (STEINBACH *and* HAMER *go up stage.*)

So you have not forgotten me? There is no
need to ask, for you would not have attacked
me as you did if you had forgotten—that we
were once friends.

REID.

I would not have you think that. It was
to disabuse your mind of such thought that I
stayed to explain—to excuse, if you will, some

excesses of language, and to assure you that I shall act with absolute impartiality towards you.

LADY ANNE.

But do you think that you can hold the balance as fairly as you propose to? Can you guard your heart so that nothing, no trifle, no bitter remembrance, shall fall into the scale against me? We are not strangers; do you think it is possible to play at being strangers?

REID.

That I cannot say; we can only endeavour to be just.

LADY ANNE.

I know there are many with you who hardly desire a settlement of this dispute, who at heart believe that the destruction of my property is the best that could happen. Ellen Sands, the young lady you are engaged to marry, is of this way of thinking, or very nearly.

REID.

I must leave Ellen to answer for herself.

LADY ANNE.

But you would not wish the strike to continue
if I could prove by my books that it would be
impossible to raise the men's wages twenty per
cent. and still work the mine at a profit?

REID.

No, I should not.   But capitalists are not in
the habit of submitting their books to strangers
—to their enemies.

LADY ANNE (*gently*).

We were once friends.   I should not mind
submitting the books of the mine to you.
When will you come and inspect them?   Will
you come to-morrow?

REID.

I can do nothing without consulting my col-
leagues.   But they will raise no objection—it
would be impossible to object.

LADY ANNE.

Then you will come to-morrow?

REID.

To-morrow? I have to speak at several places
to-morrow. But I could be here by four in the
afternoon, if that will suit you.

LADY ANNE.

That will do very well.

FOOTMAN.

Luncheon is ready, my lady.

LADY ANNE.

You will stop to lunch, I hope?

REID.

That, I regret, is quite impossible.

LADY ANNE.

Surely——

REID.

You must excuse me. (*He takes his hat and
moves towards the door.*) Good-day, Lady Anne.

LADY ANNE.

Are you going to the committee rooms?

REID.

Yes.

LADY ANNE.

Then your shortest way will be through the garden.   I will show you the way.

> (REID *hesitates;* STEINBACH *and* HAMER *watch him.   He follows* LADY ANNE *through the window.*)

HAMER.

Lady Anne seems of a very forgiving disposition.   If one had not been present at the deputation one would think they were old friends.

STEINBACH.

They are old friends.   He was her father's secretary ten years ago.   It is said that she broke his heart——

HAMER.

What a remarkable story!   It is quite dramatic. . . .   I don't suppose Lady Anne would mind my writing an article about it. (*Pause.*)   The facts are well known, I suppose?

STEINBACH (*going towards the door*).

Such a matter could not be discussed in a public print.

HAMER.

But really——

STEINBACH (*opening the door*).

No, Mr. Hamer, I cannot minister to journalistic curiosity.

(*Exit* HAMER.　STEINBACH *goes towards the window.*)

CURTAIN.

ACT II.

SCENE.—*The same as before, Lady Anne's drawing-room.* LADY ANNE *discovered.* STEINBACH *enters, right.*

LADY ANNE.

You have finished with the books?

STEINBACH.

Yes.

LADY ANNE.

And they prove all we said?

STEINBACH.

Yes, and something more.

LADY ANNE.

Then surely I did right in wanting John Reid to inspect the books; once convinced of the impossibility of the miners' demands, he will surely not persevere in an adventure that must end in our mutual ruin—my ruin and their ruin.

STEINBACH.

He will understand that this is so ; the testimony of the books is convincing. But I fail to see how the mere opening of Mr. Reid's eyes will alter things.

LADY ANNE.

Then you don't believe in Mr. Reid's honesty ?

STEINBACH.

On the contrary, I believe him to be an honest man and a clever man ! But that is not sufficient. I had an opportunity of studying him the other day.

LADY ANNE.

What do you mean ?

STEINBACH.

I may be wrong, but this is what I think ! You take Reid for a force ! I take him for an eloquent interpreter of a force. Let us suppose that an examination of the books convinces him

5

of the folly of the men's demands, and that
forthwith he goes into the market-place and
says—" My poor fellows, I was mistaken, and
my advice to you now is to go back to work."

LADY ANNE.

You think they will not take his advice? But
yesterday you saw that he had only to raise his
voice and the men followed like sheep.

STEINBACH.

He was then appealing to their brutish
instincts; telling them that their homes were
not so comfortable as your drawing-room.
Besides, you have forgotten Ellen Sands.

LADY ANNE.

You think that it will be impossible to convince her?

STEINBACH.

Her beliefs are not swayed by facts and
figures; they are well entrenched in pure theory,
and are practically inaccessible to argument.

LADY ANNE.

Then you think that John Reid's examination of the books will come to nothing ?

STEINBACH.

Something comes of everything, but what? Briefly, I do not think that this inspection of the books will prove as easy a solution of your difficulties as you imagine.

LADY ANNE.

But I did not propose this inspection of books until you had failed.

STEINBACH.

Failed !   A little vulgar rhetoric answered by a few idiotic cheers; a few caps thrown into the air. Had I had my way, those caps and cheers would have been instantly answered by a withdrawal of your offer of five per cent. But instead, you threw yourself on the man's mercy; you capitulated without terms—you invited him here. This policy may prove successful. He loved you when you were a girl; you come with all the added charms of womanhood. He may lose his head ; you may twist him round your finger, but the step is a perilous one.

LADY ANNE.

Why perilous for me ?

STEINBACH.

Supposing your names were scandalously connected together—your name and the name of a socialist leader !   Think of it ; all help from your family would be at an end.   Your father, Lord Elwin, who might assist you——

LADY ANNE.

But you'll tell no one of our boy and girl flirtation—that silly love-story which I told you of.

STEINBACH.

When you took Reid through the garden, that newspaper fellow—Hamer is his name, I think— and I were standing by the window—you passed out before us.

LADY ANNE.

But you told him nothing !

STEINBACH.

I had to say something. I told him that Reid had been your father's secretary. It seemed the least compromising thing I could say.

LADY ANNE.

I wish you hadn't done this!

STEINBACH.

I had to say something.

LADY ANNE.

It was wrong of me; I didn't think of what I was doing. If it becomes known it will irritate that girl Ellen Sands still further against me. If I fail it will be through her. She'll prove my stumbling-block.

STEINBACH.

Then woman proves woman's stumbling-block as well as man's.

LADY ANNE.

Oh! Edward, let me be! This is no time for epigrams—ruin hangs like a sword above me. The overseers are working fifteen hours a day.

Only this morning I heard that they will not be able to bear the strain much longer; the mine will be flooded, and I shall be ruined! Oh! it is cruel! Why was I selected? Why do they attack a woman? Why do they choose the weakest?

STEINBACH.

The weakest is Nature's instinctive selection. It is the weakest that goes to the wall first. (*Seeing there are tears in* LADY ANNE'S *eyes, his manner softens.*) But why does the weak refuse association with the strong? Dearest Anne, you know that my fortune as well as my heart is at your disposal. (*Takes her in his arms and kisses her.*)

LADY ANNE.

Money, my dear Baron, has never influenced my choice. We may be worldly and not as good as we might be, but for our sakes we must keep ourselves free from that taint. I told you yesterday that I was in too great trouble to think of love or lovers. After the battle, who knows? During the battle I want you to be my friend.

STEINBACH.

Well, let it be so.   I'll be your friend, and if chance should favour me I shall deem myself the most fortunate of men.

LADY ANNE.

Is this a compact ?

STEINBACH.

Yes; and I should be satisfied if I thought, if I were sure, you didn't care for this socialist chief.

LADY ANNE.

I in love with John Reid!   How absurd!

STEINBACH.

It does seem absurd, but I half fancied that this socialist chief—this man you had loved long ago, who comes up to you from an unknown world, halo of poetry about him—had inspired in you some sort of fantastic caprice, some sort of capricious interest.

LADY ANNE (*absent-mindedly*).

No, I'm not in love with John Reid; that is

all over and done with. He hates me. If you were to ask him, he would describe me as a cruel, heartless woman. I did treat him cruelly, I know I did; but it was not all my fault. He's now going to marry Ellen Sands. Oh, no, I'm not in love with him. That is quite an absurd idea.

STEINBACH.

Sweetheart, swear that you do not love him.

LADY ANNE.

I do not care for him.

STEINBACH.

Then you'll love me. You once did—you will again. (*Putting his arms round her.* LADY ANNE *moves away.*)

LADY ANNE.

Hush, some one's coming.
    (*The door opens and servant announces that* JOHN REID *is downstairs.*)

FOOTMAN.

Mr. John Reid wishes to see your ladyship. Is your ladyship at home?

STEINBACH.

My advice is not to receive him.

LADY ANNE.

I cannot do that. What excuse can I give?

STEINBACH.

Excuse! The usual excuse—a sick headache.

LADY ANNE.

He wouldn't believe it. It would only incense him still further against me. I must see him. (*To Servant.*) Show Mr. Reid up.

(*Exit Servant.*)

Believe me that I do this only in the hope of obtaining a settlement of this dispute.

STEINBACH.

In the hope of alienating him from his party?

LADY ANNE.

Yes; that is my only reason. I shall expect you this evening to dinner, and will tell you all

about it. (STEINBACH *looks at her doubtfully.*
REID *enters. The men bow to each other.*)

REID (*a suspicion of shyness*).

I'm afraid I'm disturbing you. You're engaged, I see.

LADY ANNE.

Not at all ; Baron Steinbach was just leaving.
He's been good enough to put my books in
order. He has explained them to me so that
I can explain them to you.

STEINBACH.

Your books are excellently well kept ; they
can be read at a glance. But perhaps a lady
and a poet will not read them as easily as a
financier.

REID.

I've had some practice with accounts, and
unless they're very difficult indeed, I shall be
able to understand them. Poets are not such
impracticable beings as financiers imagine.

LADY ANNE.

Mr. Reid's poetry is as well known to the

world as his socialism.   The world prefers his
poetry.

REID.

One half the world.

STEINBACH.

A strange alliance, poetry and socialism; and
yet I don't know, in the modern world mysticism
finds expression in socialism and science.

REID.

Mysticism!   So we seem to you like mystics
a recrudescence of the Middle Ages.   And you
wonder if we really believe that the future will
differ from the present.

STEINBACH.

I certainly wonder that an intelligence like
yours should never doubt the possibility of
man's regeneration.

REID.

You believe man to be utterly base.

STEINBACH.

The mass of mankind, certainly.

REID.

A cruel creed, an ignoble creed. I could not live if I did not hold to some hope of earthly salvation.

STEINBACH.

I wonder if your speech comes from conviction, or if it is a mere habit of eloquence. There is one question that I put to men like you. If the capitalists were abolished to-morrow, tell me what you would do with the incorrigibly idle; those who would say, " We will not work, we prefer to beg," and wander the world over.

REID.

Not long ago I met an old couple on a country road. They had worked forty years in the factory; they could work no more, and were on their way to the Poor-house; yet Baron Steinbach wonders why the poor are not more industrious.

STEINBACH.

In every system there must be failures.

REID.

You think that the successes of the system should reconcile us to its failures?

STEINBACH.

There is neither present nor past system; it is human passion that blocks your way. But argument is useless. Lady Anne, the accounts are in the library.

LADY ANNE.

I shall expect you to dinner at eight, Baron.

STEINBACH.

I'm not leaving. I've some letters to write. I shall find what I want in the morning-room.

(*Exit.*)

REID.

A strange man. He seems to take pleasure in the knowledge that evil exists.

LADY ANNE.

He's a man without illusions.

REID.

Has he taught you to think like him?

LADY ANNE.

No; I always try to look on the pleasant side.

(LADY ANNE *shows signs of emotion, her handkerchief is in her hand.*)

REID.

You seem troubled, Lady Anne. Perhaps you're not feeling well, and would like to postpone the examination of accounts?

LADY ANNE.

No, I'm well enough. Even so, I should not allow health to interfere, however distraught I may feel.

REID.

Distraught!

LADY ANNE.

The difficulty of knowing what to do, how to act. Whatever course I take, it seems to be the wrong one.

REID.

I think you have acted wisely in submitting to an inspection of your books. For after all it

is but a question of facts and figures. I may
say that when I reported your decision the
majority of the committee was impressed in
your favour.

LADY ANNE.

But if the books vindicate my position, do you
guarantee that the men return to work at once?

REID.

I shall certainly advise that the strike be
discontinued.

LADY ANNE.

Perhaps that advice will be opposed.

REID.

Maybe; but the extreme views do not carry
a majority of votes.

LADY ANNE.

You're alluding to Ellen Sands.

REID.

Miss Sands, I admit, holds extreme views;
but so does your friend Baron Steinbach. Ellen
Sands and Baron Steinbach represent the poles

of the social question.   Both are for war to the knife.

LADY ANNE.

Baron Steinbach anticipates Miss Sands' opposition, and says that this inspection of the books will only end in useless publication of my affairs. (*Pause.*) On certain conditions he would help me with all his wealth to fight the demands of the miners, and with his money I could not fail to force them to accept the terms I was pleased to impose.

REID.

And you have declined his aid ?

LADY ANNE.

I hesitated to accept his offer. (*Pause.*) I do not wish to crush these poor people utterly. I do not believe them to be dissatisfied with their condition ; they are merely ill-advised. Nor do I believe that the advice that they follow is altogether disinterested.

REID.

Lady Anne !

LADY ANNE.

I do not wish to accuse either you or your associates of dishonesty, but did you not tell me just now that Ellen Sands was opposed to an inspection of my books? In other words, was opposed to any amicable settlement of this dispute. Ellen Sands hates me.

REID.

No; she merely hates the class to which you belong.

LADY ANNE.

Does she know, have you told her, that we were once—well—shall I say sweethearts?

REID.

I have told her nothing. She knows nothing for certain. The flowers you left for me seemed to rouse some suspicion in her mind. But it has passed away.

LADY ANNE.

Did the perfume tell you who had left the flowers for you?

6

REID.

Not at first. I could not remember where
I had met that perfume. It seemed to recall
a far-off time, a dead past; but when I tried
to define what it did recall, the illusion vanished.
Ellen's description of you did not help me. It
was when my thoughts were occupied with
other things that the haunting odour seemed
on the point of whispering its secret. I put
the flowers away, but the soft, insinuating odour
pursued me, held me sleepless. . . . Suddenly
I cried out—"It is she!"

LADY ANNE.

I remember the day you left Torrington
Park. I saw you walk across the park in the
rain; you had told me that I had broken your
heart.

REID.

I did not speak false. You were a cruel,
heartless girl, as you are now a cruel, heartless
woman.

LADY ANNE (*dashes the tears aside*).

I am sorry you think so badly of me, but it

can't be helped. . . . I did treat you cruelly, I know.

REID.

But have we not other things to discuss?

LADY ANNE.

No; this matter demands settlement before all others. How was I circumstanced at the time? Have you forgotten that I was no more than a child, hardly seventeen, when you first told me that you loved me? I was true to my love until——

REID.

Until you realised that you could not marry your father's secretary.

LADY ANNE.

Have it so, then. Why did I seek to convince you? What is it to me how vile you think me? Still it seems to me strange that, after all these years, so clever a man should not be able to see that I was helpless in the hands of my relatives. What was my will against their will?

REID.

You made no effort to resist them. You were determined on a rich marriage.

LADY ANNE.

If I had married you, you would be tired of me by now. We should have been married ten years. All the romance would be faded.

REID.

You think so. Is that the lesson that life has taught you?

LADY ANNE.

You think, then, that you wouldn't have grown tired of me? You used to say so. I still keep the verses you wrote to me. Do you remember the corner of the terrace where the sun set behind the hills? Looking down that valley, we thought that we saw our lives from end to end.

REID.

That illusive valley.

LADY ANNE.

I like the poem.   It is one of the prettiest in
your book.   You see I have marked it.

REID.

Oh, then you have read my poems?

LADY ANNE.

Yes, I bought the volume when it first came
out.   I little thought I should meet John Reid
again and in such circumstances.

REID.

Or little cared.   I remember one evening, we
were walking together on the terrace, we had
said that we loved one another.   The conversation had fallen ; I was thinking of our future,
and without a word of warning you said,
" But this will never be."   Next time we met I
noticed that your manner was wholly changed,
and when your coldness forced me to ask you
if you wished me to forget you, to go away,
you answered, " I think it would be as well if
you did."

LADY ANNE.

It is as I thought. You remember only what was disagreeable in me. You cannot find excuse in childish ignorance. However, you have forgotten me. How could it be otherwise? what we're talking of is ten years ago.

REID.

Why do we speak of these things? (*Stops and looks at her.*) I have done nothing but reproach you. I really don't know why. I've come here on a purely business matter. Why do we not confine ourselves to it?

LADY ANNE.

Perhaps it would be better if we did. The accounts are in the library. I'll take you there at once. (*She goes towards the door. Looking round.*) But how pale you're looking, and all this time I've not asked you to sit down. . . . You're looking ill.

REID.

It is nothing. I'm only a little tired. I've been speaking in the Merton district. I'd then to attend a committee meeting. I was detained longer than I expected, and had to run most of the way here.

LADY ANNE.

I should have noticed your tired face before. Sit down—rest yourself.

REID.

I'll sit down for a few minutes—if you're not pressed for time?

LADY ANNE.

I've nothing to do. . . . But I must be careful what I talk to you about. You do not wish to speak of the past—let us speak of the present. You've made your way in the world since we last saw each other. I should like to hear how you won your success. You must have worked very hard. You must have suffered ; for you'd very little, only your younger child's portion.

REID.

I was poor then, I'm poor now—now, because my work leaves so little time for earning money. I suppose it was hard at first, but I went through no melodramatic struggle for existence. I could always make money with my pen.

LADY ANNE.

I am glad of that. Then why——

REID.

Did I become a socialist? Oh, it was not because I could not "get on."

LADY ANNE.

There must have been a reason.

REID.

Oh yes, there was a reason.

LADY ANNE.

Perhaps I shall not be able to understand your reasons? I know nothing of political economy.

REID.

My reason was a very simple one—so simple that I can hardly call it a reason at all—a mere human sentiment. I felt I was leading a selfish life. I grew aware of the misery around me. When I came home in the morning in evening clothes and white cravat I did not dare to look the poor vagrants in the face—the poor wretches who had just risen from the cold stones and walked shivering onwards in front of the policeman.

LADY ANNE.

I remember one summer morning I dropped my fan as I was getting out of the carriage. One of those poor creatures picked it up and handed it to me. It was horrible.

REID.

I came to think more and more about the poverty and the misery that three parts of the world live in—of the injustice of what we call civilisation, and gradually——

LADY ANNE.

So it was not Ellen Sands who drew you into socialism?

REID.

No; I've only known her about a year. But it was her enthusiasm that strengthened me in my convictions; I might say gave me convictions, for before I met her I only felt that things were wrong in the world. I did not know that they could be remedied.

LADY ANNE.

And now you're going to marry her; and henceforth you'll live among the people. You're going to take the final step. I wonder if you'll be happy?

REID.

I shall be happy as another. Who is happy? Are you happy?

LADY ANNE.

I often think I'm not. I often hate my life, and wonder what is the use of all this hurry after mere amusement. But I never had any one to encourage me to think, to help me to think. (*Pause.*) I like to listen to you. It seems quite natural to think as you do. It is interesting to think of things.

(*Enter* BARON STEINBACH.)

STEINBACH.

Oh, I thought you were in the library examining the books.

REID.

Lady Anne has been good enough to take an

interest in my book.   It is, I'm afraid, too easy to tempt a poet into talking of his verses.

LADY ANNE.

I'm quite ready.

REID.

But it seems a shame, Lady Anne, to fatigue you with dry account-books.   If Baron Steinbach has finished his letters——

LADY ANNE.

The accounts will not fatigue me.   Besides, this will be an opportunity to obtain an insight into my affairs, which I have neglected.   It is I who should speak to you of fatigue.   You're really looking very tired and pale.

STEINBACH.

I wonder when Mr. Reid will tire of work for those who understand nothing of his aims and aspirations, whose ideas are limited to their pint-pots !

REID.

Lady Anne, time presses.   If you wish me to

go into the matter of these accounts, I must do so at once. If the books are in order it will not take us long to get at the results.

LADY ANNE.

This is the way to the library.

(*Exeunt, right.*)

STEINBACH.

I wonder what the effect of this meeting will be—accounts and conversations about poetry. (*Paces the stage.*) Poetry !

(*Stops before table, takes up* REID'S *poems, sits down, and turns over the leaves.* FOOTMAN *opens the door; shows in* Mr. HAMER.)

HAMER.

I apologise, Baron Steinbach. I do hope I am not wasting your valuable time. But I thought you might favour me with your views on the capitalistic question before I leave Arlingford.

STEINBACH.

My dear Mr. Hamer, what can I have

to say on a subject so utterly worn out with controversy?

HAMER.

For the original mind no subject is worn out.

STEINBACH.

You're too complimentary. However, if you'll put some questions, I'll try to answer them.

HAMER.

You visited Lady Anne's mine this morning; you were impressed by its gloom, its danger. . . . Let me remind you that human beings are born for life-long labour in its subterranean night . . . How different their fate from yours! In a few weeks you'll be back in your palace on the beautiful Italian coast. I want to ask you if you think such inequality just?

STEINBACH.

Of course it is not just. Look into Nature, examine her intentions, and you'll find injustice at the root of every one. What can be more unjust than that one brother should never know a day's illness, and the other brother should never know a day's health? Why do some come into the world criminals, crazed with passion from which they cannot escape, and which lead them by certain steps to the gallows?

HAMER.

The socialists know very well that there will always be healthy and unhealthy, stupid and intelligent, but they think that——

STEINBACH.

That some day they'll be neither rich nor poor? But poverty and riches are merely the consequence of health and disease, stupidity and intelligence.

HAMER.

If it were not legal for the individual to accumulate capital there would be neither rich nor poor.

STEINBACH.

But it is nature and not man that is the inexorable tyrant. (*Getting up, holding on to and leaning over the rail of his chair.*) You want me to tell you what I think of the capitalistic system. The capitalistic system is founded on thrift, on industry, and on forethought—three things which the world has agreed to call virtues. It is also founded on the lust of possession, on the pleasure of gambling, and the craving for personal superiority—three things which the world has agreed to call vices. Do you think that a system, founded on six instincts inherited from the beginning of time, can be overthrown?

HAMER.

Then you think that our present form of civilisation will endure for ever—that we have reached the highest attainable point?

STEINBACH.

New combinations will arise, but nothing will be altered. There have been a thousand reformers and not a single reformation. The misery of man is incurable.

HAMER.

Do you go so far as to say that life subsists

on misery and vice as much as on happiness and virtue?

STEINBACH.

Surely. Misery and vice are antecedent to capital; they exist because Nature believes them essential in her design.

HAMER (*writing, and speaking to himself*).

Man cannot live by virtue alone.

STEINBACH.

Precisely; man cannot live by virtue alone. Nature and the socialist are at variance on this point, and Nature does not allow any one to contradict her. Socialism would take from life all it has of adventure and excitement; it would reduce the world to the colourless void of monastic life. It would go further than the most ferocious ascetic has yet gone; it would take from life even the excitement of religion! In the socialist monastery gambling for places in Paradise would not be allowed. (*Turning to* HAMER.) Have you got that?

HAMER.

One moment. (*He finishes writing and looks up.*) But would you deny progress altogether? Surely the world is not as ignorant as it was? Education——

STEINBACH.

Education! What has it done? You've taught men to read, but what do they read? Are the books written to-day, when every one knows how to read, better than those that were written two thousand years ago, when few knew how to read? You have established schools for instruction in the art of painting and sculpture. Are your painting and sculpture as good as the painting and sculpture done before the world had begun to indulge in dreams of educational advantages?

HAMER.

You must admit that there is at least one improvement in modern over ancient life—the abolition of slavery.

STEINBACH.

The argument of the socialists is that the

7

factory is the most ferocious form of slavery that the world has ever known. And I'm not sure that they are not right.

HAMER (*getting up and closing his note-book*).

There are two more questions I should like to ask you, Baron Steinbach. You're said to be one of the richest men in the world. The other day I saw it stated that your fortune exceeded ten millions.

STEINBACH.

Ten millions ! When a man is known to be rich he's credited with ten—a thousand times his real wealth. But let the amount be waived. What do you want to ask me ?

HAMER.

I want to ask you if money is happiness?

STEINBACH (*walking up the stage*).

Oh, no. Happiness is another thing. Money, of course, means a great deal, otherwise we should not take the trouble we do to acquire it.

But happiness is found not in money, but in work.

HAMER.

My last question.

STEINBACH.

Ask it.

HAMER.

Admitting your contention that all are at liberty to acquire capital, and that capital is acquired by the intelligent and the industrious, do you not think that it is unjust that a man should be allowed to leave his money to children who have not worked for it, and are perhaps neither intelligent nor industrious?

STEINBACH (*coming down the stage*).

Are you married?

HAMER.

No, not yet.

STEINBACH.

When you are, and have children, believe me you'll not question the law of inheritance.

HAMER.

I understand. The family is the rock on which socialism goes to pieces. Thank you very much, Baron Steinbach. Your views, I'm sure, will be read with great interest. I will send you a copy of the paper. I suppose that this address will find you. But that reminds me : you remember the interesting details you were kind enough to supply me with regarding the romantic attachment of Lady Anne and John Reid in early life?

STEINBACH.

I hope you've not referred to that in your paper.

HAMER.

Well, you remember I asked you if the facts were known?

STEINBACH.

I said that the story was not one that could be discussed in a public print. It will injure Reid's position.

HAMER.

It may do that ; but, you see, it was a really interesting item of news, and things are so dull at present. I think you'll find that I've treated the subject delicately. I do hope Lady Anne will not be annoyed.

STEINBACH.

She certainly will be annoyed. I'm afraid you cannot come here again.

HAMER.

I'm sure I should be sorry to think that—but it's too late now. (*Preparing to go.*)

STEINBACH.

Has your article appeared ?

HAMER.

No, but I'm afraid it is too late to withdraw it. It will probably go into to-morrow's or Wednesday's paper. I'll send it to you, and I hope you'll tell Lady Anne that——

STEINBACH.

I'll tell her what you say—that things were dull. But I doubt if she'll be able to see the matter in that light.

HAMER.

Thank you for your very interesting views—most interesting, I'm sure. Thank you again, and good morning.   (*Exit.*)

STEINBACH (*returning from the door*).

I thought that he would not be able to resist the temptation. I think that his article will bring this ridiculous flirtation to an end. (*Goes to door at back. As he lays his hand on the handle, enter* LADY ANNE *and* REID.)

STEINBACH.

Ah, so you've finished with the books. I hope they've convinced you——

REID.

Of the impracticability of our demands? Quite.

STEINBACH.

I'm glad of that. It says much for your open-mindedness.

LADY ANNE.

Mr. Reid will advise the discontinuation of the strike?

REID.

I shall report the result of my examination of your books—the figures speak for themselves.

STEINBACH.

This is a serious refutation of your ideas.

(*Enter* FOOTMAN.)

FOOTMAN (*approaching* BARON STEINBACH).

Mr. Hamer has come back, sir, and wishes to know if he can have a word with you.

LADY ANNE.

Will you see him in the morning-room, Baron Steinbach? Mr. Reid and——

REID.

But my business is quite finished. Pray do
not let me——

LADY ANNE.

Mr. Reid, I hope you are not going yet.
We've still——

STEINBACH.

Will you excuse me? One has never quite
done with an interviewer. I'll see you later on,
Lady Anne.   (*Exit.*)

REID.

I see that Baron Steinbach is an intimate
friend of yours.

LADY ANNE.

I've known him a long while, and when all
this trouble came I wrote asking him to help
me. He came at once.

REID.

Was it love of you or hatred of us that
brought him to Arlingford, I wonder?

LADY ANNE.

It is difficult to say why men do things. But you see that I preferred to accept your help to his.

REID.

I daresay he advised you against me—against this course. I remember you told me he did.

LADY ANNE.

He doubts your power to assist me. He says you'll be opposed ; he thinks you'll not be able to overcome this opposition.

REID.

What opposition ? That of that thick-headed fellow the secretary of the committee, and a few fanatics ? He's mistaken. I've a hold over the men that they haven't. Ellen knows them all ; they're her friends, she visits them in their homes ; but when it comes to a pinch it is I whom they obey.

LADY ANNE.

I wonder how that is ? You're so different—

you haven't a thought, not a sympathy in common.

REID.

I beg your pardon. At heart I was always of the people. They care little for poetry, it is true. But their sturdy fighting manhood is common ground where hearts—and fists too !—may meet. The other day I took off my coat and gave a fellow a hiding. You should have heard them cheer me. My popularity is ten times what it was. I can do what I like with them.

LADY ANNE.

You gave the fellow a thrashing. Tell me about it.

REID.

It was about the right to trade away the stores that had been obtained with the tickets— something about the tickets, something about drink. They must accept your last offer. Let me see, the percentage is — I've forgotten. My memory's gone. (*Sinks into a chair.*)

LADY ANNE.

Oh, what is this? (*Supports his head with her*

arm.) He's fainted ; he's seriously ill. (*Runs for scent, wets her pocket handkerchief, and bathes his face. He begins to revive.*) He has only fainted. John, speak to me. Are you better ? Lie still. No, no. Let me bathe your temples.

REID.

What is it—Anne, Anne ! it is you ?   Tell me what has happened. (*Pause.*)   I fainted, didn't I ? (*He closes his eyes.*)

LADY ANNE.

He's fainted again.

REID.

No, I haven't. But my head is swimming. I was saying something to you. What did I say ? Did I tell you that——

LADY ANNE.

You said nothing.

REID.

Ah ! that perfume, how it brings back the

past! I was writing all last night, and I ate nothing—I had no time. I have overdone it; that's all.

LADY ANNE.

You mustn't talk. Rest——

REID.

I'm better now. (*Makes an effort to rise.*)

LADY ANNE.

Let me help you. (*She helps him to rise.*)

REID (*leaning against the table*).

Fainting like a girl. I'm ashamed of myself. I shall be all right when I get into the air. Good-bye, Lady Anne. You'll excuse me.

LADY ANNE.

But you're not going yet. Wait until you're better.

REID.

May I have a glass of water?

LADY ANNE.

I'll ring for one. (*Rings. The* FOOTMAN *enters. To* FOOTMAN.) Bring a glass of water at once—quickly. (*Exit* FOOTMAN.) Let me order you some lunch; you're starving !

REID.

A glass of water will be sufficient. It is only a little faintness. I shall be all right presently. (*Enter* FOOTMAN *with water.* REID *drinks. Exit* FOOTMAN. REID *prepares to go.*)

LADY ANNE.

You must take more care of yourself; your health will break down if you don't. I suppose we've said everything. But you'll find time to come and see me again. I'm not the superficial woman you take me for. I want to hear your ideas. When will you come and see me ?

REID.

There would be no reason for my coming here again. You forget how different are our positions. Besides, the turn that events have taken will leave little spare time on my hands. I must now consider the best way of getting the men back to work.

LADY ANNE.

But you must not think that it was for that I invited you here.

REID.

Surely.

LADY ANNE.

You think there was no other reason?

REID.

Perhaps you felt some sort of interest in seeing me again.

LADY ANNE.

Indeed I did. I asked you here because I want you to forgive me. (*Giving him her hands.*)

REID.

I wish we had met in other circumstances.

LADY ANNE.

Circumstances do not control those who care
for each other.

REID.

Care for each other !

LADY ANNE.

When you fainted just now I learnt from your
own lips that you loved me.   You do love me ;
you cannot deny it.

REID.

Alas ! I've never loved any one but you.   It
is too late now.

LADY ANNE.

It is never too late.   I, too, have a confession
to make.   I have not forgotten you.   I never
loved any one but you.

REID.

Ah, I heard you say the same words long ago,
and I learnt what your love was worth.

LADY ANNE.

I am not situated as I was then.

REID.

Nor was I situated then as I am now.

LADY ANNE.

Do you doubt my love? Why should I tell you so if it were not true?

REID.

Why indeed!

LADY ANNE.

It is your duty to tell the men to return to work. Only revenge could prevent you from doing so, and you do not want revenge, do you?

REID.

Anne, it is too late; my troth is pledged to another.

LADY ANNE.

To whom? You do not love that threadpaper girl with theories instead of blood in her veins ?

REID.

Not as I once loved you.

LADY ANNE.

Nor even as you love me now. (*She draws herself against him like a cat.*) Kiss me! (*He kisses her and breaks away from her. He stands looking into space; she sits down, right. Pause.*)

REID.

You want me to betray her as once you betrayed me. To cause her the same suffering. This can only end in shame and ruin. (*With sudden determination.*) I will go at once. (*Exit.*)

LADY ANNE.

Gone, gone! I shall never see him again. She'll never let him come here again. (*Throws herself on the sofa.*) Ah, I could have loved that man. (*Getting up.*) I must, I will . . . I shall see him again. I will write to him. (*Goes to writing-table. Two minutes should elapse between* REID'S *exit and his*

8

entrance. The door opens; REID *enters, a letter in his hand.*) Ah, so you've come back. What has brought you back? Something has happened. Bad news is written in your face.

REID.

The worst of news. Irrevocable disaster !

LADY ANNE.

What do you mean? Tell me.

REID.

As I was leaving, this letter was put into my hand. (*Reading.*) " Sir,—Knowing the situation to be critical in Arlingford, I send you a cheque for £2000. It is necessary that labour should win this battle. Arlingford is the key to the situation in the North.—A friend of labour." A friend of labour? Ah, a cruel friend ! (*Clenching letter.*) Ah ! it is you who have destroyed us.

LADY ANNE.

But you'll tell the miners that the books prove that their demands are impossible, that to continue the strike must end in the ruin of my property — of their property. You will appeal to their reason.

REID.

With this money in my hand it were idle to advise them to return to work.

LADY ANNE.

Then I'm ruined, utterly ruined! (*They sit down*, REID *in a chair next the table*, LADY ANNE *in a chair down the stage on the right.*) When the money is gone, when they would return to work, the property which cost the labour of three generations to create will have disappeared ; the mine will be a swamp.

REID.

Yes, a vast property lost to a little drunkenness ! What a derision ! (*Getting up, and going to* LADY ANNE.) But cannot you get money from your relations sufficient to keep the mine in working order ?

LADY ANNE.

My relations cannot help me; no one can help me now, except Baron Steinbach.

REID.

Baron Steinbach! (LADY ANNE *looks at him. Recollecting himself.*) Baron Steinbach, our bitterest foe; he would crush us with his millions! He would resist until he forced the poor folk to accept his terms; God knows what they'd be! The alternative is a terrible one, but I do not understand why you have not already accepted his help.

LADY ANNE.

Let us say because I do not wish to crush these poor people utterly; give me credit for some good intention.

REID (*taking her hands*).

Is this really true, Anne?

LADY ANNE.

Yes, it is quite true. There is one way out of this terrible situation. No one knows of the

arrival of that cheque; say nothing about it, and
advise the men to return to work.

REID.

Detain this cheque, and advise the men to
return to work!   You do not realise what you
are asking!

LADY ANNE.

Yes, I do.   Detain that cheque a few days—a
few hours may be sufficient.   Tell them to go
back to work; save them, and save me!

REID.

"To do a great right to do a little wrong."
But is my wrong little, however noble my
purpose.   One cannot foresee the end of such
an act.   Oh, God! my responsibility is greater
than I can bear!

LADY ANNE.

Save them from Steinbach!   Save me!

REID.

I'll save you both!   (*To himself.*)   And will

bear the punishment even if it falls upon me both sides.

LADY ANNE.

You do this for me, for me who did you such wrong? How can I thank you, how can I recompense you? Say that you forgive me the past!

REID.

Let me not think that it is for you I do this.

LADY ANNE.

Why should it not be for me?

REID.

Were it so, it would be a shameful act.

LADY ANNE.

Shameful to save the woman you once loved from ruin.

REID.

Ah, if it should become known that I once loved you, no other explanation except love of you will be believed.

LADY ANNE.

Then you hesitate—you're afraid?

REID.

No, I am not afraid. I'll do this. But we must not meet again. (*He gets up to go.* LADY ANNE *stands between him and the door.*)

LADY ANNE.

We must not meet again.

CURTAIN.

ACT III.

SCENE.—*The same as before. Lady Anne's drawing-room. As the curtain rises,* LADY ANNE *is seating herself on the sofa.* REID *is standing by her.*

LADY ANNE.

At last we're alone. The worst of servants is that one can't speak before them, unless one speaks in French. You don't, do you? Come and sit down.

(*Enter* FOOTMAN *with coffee and liqueurs.* REID *takes chair.*)

Oh, here's the coffee. (*To* FOOTMAN.) You can put it on that table. I will serve it. (FOOT-MAN *draws over the wicker table, and places coffee upon it. Exit* FOOTMAN. LADY ANNE *puts her hands on* REID'S *shoulders and looks at him.*) I cannot imagine how you could have ever thought of marrying a woman who wasn't a lady.

REID.

Why introduce a subject that you know must be painful to me? Let us not speak of Ellen.

LADY ANNE.

I'm jealous of her, of the influence she has had over you. You never could have lived among common people. Admit that you're glad to find yourself in a drawing-room again.

REID.

Among the refinements of life! I never regretted these things, I only regretted you. (*Enter* FOOTMAN; *offers liqueurs.*) None, thank you.

LADY ANNE.

What, no liqueur; not even a glass of Chartreuse? What an ascetic you've become! (*Exit* FOOTMAN.) At last we're alone. How nice it is to have you here! Tell me how you managed to get away.

REID.

It was difficult. I had to avoid exciting any suspicion.

LADY ANNE.

You're sure you weren't followed ?

REID.

Quite.

LADY ANNE.

Tell me how you managed to deceive them. I love the excitement, the intrigue ; it is half the charm.

REID.

I told them I was going for a long walk in the country. I walked for a couple of miles, until I made sure I wasn't followed, and then I took a short cut across the fields, and entered the town by the other side. That is all. And you, how did you manage to get rid of Baron Steinbach ?

LADY ANNE.

Oh, that's rather a good story. I wrote him a nice letter, inviting him to tea. I slipped a tea-gown over my dress, and with the help of some violet powder got myself up to look like an invalid. He found me lying on the sofa, a bottle of smelling salts in my hand, hardly able to speak. I gave him a cup of tea, and told him I was going to spend the evening in my room. Wasn't that ingenious?

REID.

It seems so strange that you should take this trouble for me, and after all these years.

LADY ANNE.

Why is it strange? I'll not have you look at your muddy boots. I like your loose necktie and your rough clothes; you're far nicer like that. A west-end tailor could only make you look like any other young man. No, I don't think a west-end tailor could make you look like that.

REID.

It is the novelty of my roughness that attracts, and when the spice of the novelty is worn off you'll grow tired of me, as you did before.

LADY ANNE.

Now don't begin to analyse, or you'll spoil everything.

REID.

I analyse nothing. I only know that I am yours, that you can do what you will with me. I am no longer John Reid—I am your lover.

LADY ANNE.

And you don't desire any longer to address miners at the street corner, to urge them to destroy everything beautiful in the world? You're content to sit here by me, to be my lover?

REID.

I forget all but you.   I look on your face, I watch the colour of your eyes, I hold you in my arms.

LADY ANNE.

And when you go away from here do you forget me?

REID.

Then I'm really yours . . . words, looks, everything is remembered.   I lose myself in memories of you.   There never was a more complete abandonment of self.

LADY ANNE.

I don't think your love is a selfish love.   I must prove worthy of it.

REID.

Anne, if you'd only been true to me! Ah, how I loved you! Do you remember those beautiful summer evenings by the river-side? How young we were then! Life had not had its way with us. Do you remember the oak wood and the tree on which I carved your name?

LADY ANNE.

I remember everything, John. When I read your poems all that past came back to me; the book used to fall on my knees, and I wondered if we were to meet, if you'd care for me.

REID.

But when you heard that I headed the strike on your mine, you hated me.

LADY ANNE.

No; I only thought of seeing you again. But you hated me when you came into this room at the head of the deputation. I was madly anxious to find some excuse to speak with you alone. When I caught your eye and you came down to speak to me——

REID.

You knew that you would succeed in winning
me back.

LADY ANNE.

I hoped that we might be friends.   I felt that
I must speak to you of the old days, that was
all!   And you, when did you begin to love me?

REID.

I hardly know.   It was like the giddiness
that takes a man on a cliff's edge.   I knew
that if I looked I should throw myself into
the void.   And I looked——

LADY ANNE (*freeing herself from his embrace*).

How despondent and philosophical you are!
You take life very sadly.   (*Showing her fan.*)
Look at these lovers, how gay and delightful
they are!   What do you think of my fan?   This
is an heirloom, a real old Pompadour fan, one
of Watteau's designs.   Ah! that is a century I
should have liked to live in.

REID.

Anne, listen.   I've come to tell you——

LADY ANNE.

You've come to tell me that you love me.
I won't hear anything else.   Look at my fan,
see the ladies and gallants how they're grouped
under the colonnade.   That little woman in the
brown dress, isn't she sweet?   And the little
gallant at her feet, he's nice too.   He doesn't
believe much in what he's saying; it's just part
of the entertainment.

REID.

But, Anne, do you hate deep feeling?   Must
all love be light?

LADY ANNE.

I really don't know.   You find fault with all
my conversation.   You argue everything.

REID.

Forgive me, Anne. . . . In other circumstances you would find me different.

LADY ANNE (*extending her hand to him*).

Forgive me. Go and get your poems, they are on that table; read to me.

(*He fetches book and reads.*)

REID.

One night Temptation came to me
    And woke me with her passing hair,
And led me captive by the sea,
    Adown the cliffs to the sea's lair.
The rank grass rustled sharply, stirred
    By puffing winds that gasped and died,
And through the sundered rocks was heard
    The hollow bellow of the tide.

She sate me on a narrow ledge,
    And watched me till I could not bear
Her eyes green spell. Upon the edge
    Of life she held me; in despair
I took my soul from out my heart
    And let it go for good or ill—
For why restrain what would depart;
    This soul was weary of my will.

Do you know the poem of which that is the two first stanzas?

LADY ANNE.

Yes; it is called "The Ballad of a Lost Soul." The soul wanders over the skies unable to choose among the many stars, until at last Venus rises, and then the soul is caught within the attraction of Venus.

REID.

It is strange that I should have opened this book at that poem. You do not perceive the allegory.

LADY ANNE.

I suppose you mean that I tempted you from honour and duty? Very well, go to Ellen Sands. I'm not accustomed to these hesitations; nor do I think much of those who never know their own minds, or even on what side they're fighting.

REID (*getting up*).

Anne, I beg of you to be patient with me. It is not my fault if, on entering this room, I

9

cannot efface from my mind what I have seen during the day.

LADY ANNE.

To-morrow the men will surrender; they cannot hold out much longer.

REID.

Perhaps; but this morning their sullen determined faces frightened me. I made every appeal, and failed to move them.

LADY ANNE.

How do you account for this obstinacy? Last week you had only to speak for them to obey.

REID.

Now Ellen Sands and others are against me. Besides, that article in the *Durham Mercury* telling of our early love-story has done much to undermine my influence. This morning there was talk of promised assistance and unaccountable delay in the transmission of money.

LADY ANNE.

Ah! that newspaper article. The letters I have received. It seems that at Torrington Park you're looked upon as my acknowledged lover. I, too, have made sacrifices, but I'm not so eloquent about them as you.

REID.

Anne, my position is a terrible one.

LADY ANNE.

Are you afraid?

REID.

You mean personal fear? I'm not afraid. But my guilt burns in my heart. Let me give them their money.

LADY ANNE.

To achieve my ruin your friend would see the men die by inches.

REID.

Anne, you do not know the abject suffering
of the town, and all within a few yards of you.
Let me show you. (*He leads her to window,
left.*) Look into the street. Those men are
starving. That man, how miserable he seems—
his slouching, hungry gait! And those children
who follow their mother. She has no bread to
give them. A little lath and plaster between
this elegant boudoir and miserable garrets.
Anne, have mercy!

LADY ANNE.

The night is chill, and I cannot remain by
this window. (*She wraps herself in her scarf,
and they come down the stage and sit at
table.*)

REID.

Little children in empty rooms crying for
bread. The thought is unbearable. The next
time the clock strikes I may be a murderer.
Anne, Anne! (*Throws himself on his knees.*)
Let me beg mercy of you. I beg mercy of you.

LADY ANNE.

What am I to say? The situation is a terrible one, I know. (*Buries her face in her hands.*) I am not the cruel, heartless woman you think me. I wouldn't walk over a fly on the ground if I could help it. But what am I to do? Did you not say yourself, that to surrender this money would bring ruin on the miners?

REID.

Yes. (*Getting up.*) That is the tragedy of the whole thing, the horror of the situation. But in my heart I know, Anne, that I would not have detained that cheque if I had not loved you.

LADY ANNE.

Then you regret?

REID.

That I love you? I might as well regret that I breathe, that I was born. My fear is to lose you. Then I should have realised nothing.

LADY ANNE.

Perhaps we ought never to have met.   I have
ruined you.   What will be the end of all this?

REID.

Let us go away from here; let the cheque be
acknowledged.   We are not answerable for the
catastrophe the miners bring upon themselves.
I'll work for you.   I cannot give you back your
lost wealth, but I can give you a competence.
I beseech you, Anne, do this for me; if not for
their sake, for the sake of my love.   I want to
love you, to love you always.

LADY ANNE.

You want me to fly with you, to leave everything.   (REID *takes her hands.*)   It would be
nice to go far away, to some beautiful country
—far from this trouble.   I think we could love
one another.

REID.

I have often dreamed such a love-story.   Is it
possible that my dream will be realised?

LADY ANNE.

Ah! if I could leave everything for you! Society, friends, riches—but can I? You forget what all this means to me.

REID.

I have abandoned all things for you. Honour and truth, and that pity for humanity which was once so dear to me.

LADY ANNE.

We cannot abandon the life we were brought up in. You tried to, but you've come back to it.

REID.

Anne, your fortune is in desperate peril. You're no longer sure that Baron Steinbach will help you. What will you do if you find yourself utterly ruined?

LADY ANNE.

You mean if I were left worth nothing, and had to think of—I don't say of earning my bread, but being very poor—two or three hundred a year.

REID.

If you loved me you would not hesitate.

LADY ANNE.

I do love you, but this is folly. I cannot even think of myself as a poor woman—it is impossible. I should commit suicide.

REID.

Suicide!

LADY ANNE.

Why not? I'm not afraid of death. It is so easy to die. (*Going to cabinet.*) Last year a favourite dog of mine had to be destroyed. (*Shows a small bottle.*) A few of these white grains, and the poor brute leaped up in the air and fell stone dead.

REID.

And if to-morrow you found yourself ruined you would—you shall not. (*He snatches the bottle.*)

LADY ANNE.

Give me that, you've no right to——

(*The* FOOTMAN *enters.*)

FOOTMAN.

Miss Sands is downstairs, your ladyship. She wants to see Mr. Reid.

LADY ANNE (*to* REID).

I must say that you're not here.

REID.

Is not that piling falsehood upon falsehood ?

LADY ANNE.

Very well, go to her. But before you go, do not forget that you've to make a restitution to me. Give me what you took from me just now.

REID.

Let him say that I'm not here.

LADY ANNE (*to* FOOTMAN).

Tell Miss Sands that Mr. Reid is not here,

that he left an hour ago. (*Exit* FOOTMAN.) How did they discover you were here? You must have been followed.

REID.

What can she have come for? If news of the cheque has reached them I'm lost.

LADY ANNE.

But you'll admit nothing, for my sake, to save me.

REID.

Anne, this is ruin. The detention of the cheque must be discovered. You asked for a few hours' delay—nearly a week has passed.

LADY ANNE.

To-morrow the men will surrender.

REID.

Children are starving, Anne. You've not seen their haggard faces. Anne, let that cheque be acknowledged—let us go away together.

LADY ANNE.

What folly, what folly this is!

(*Enter* FOOTMAN.)

FOOTMAN.

Miss Sands says she knows Mr. Reid is here, and refuses to leave until she has seen him.

LADY ANNE.

I dare not have her turned out.   (*To* REID.) Dare I trust you with her; are you sure that she'll not win you from me?

REID.

No one can win me from you.

LADY ANNE.

But she'll speak to you of honour, duty!

REID.

You're my only duty.

LADY ANNE (*to* FOOTMAN).

Show Miss Sands up.   (*Exit* FOOTMAN.) What can she have come for?

REID.

She may have come to question——

(*Enter* ELLEN SANDS.)

ELLEN.

I apologise, Lady Anne, for my intrusion. . . . You'll readily believe that it is as disagreeable for me to come as for you to receive me.

(LADY ANNE *affects occupation with some wool-work.*)

LADY ANNE.

Won't you sit down, Miss Sands?

ELLEN.

I'm an intruder.   Only the most important business could have brought me here, therefore there's no reason why I should sit down.

LADY ANNE.

As you like, Miss Sands.   I didn't wish you to seem as if you'd come after a situation, that's all.   Your business is important, and you see the hour is late.

ELLEN.

And yet Mr. Reid is here.

LADY ANNE.

Mr. Reid and I are old friends, as I believe you're aware. He's been dining here. . . . You see I continue to answer your questions.

ELLEN.

Dining here!—one of the few houses where there has been dinner to-night. The town is starving. Ah, the poor little children crying for bread . . . wild work may happen before morning.

REID.

This morning I besought the men to relinquish the hopeless struggle, but you and others opposed my advice. You insisted that the books of capitalists could not be trusted, that to go back to work unless every demand was acceded to was to go back to slavery. Therefore I say, Ellen, let the guilt be upon your head—the suffering endured and the acts it may bring about.

ELLEN.

I do not hesitate to accept the responsibility. The fate of unborn generations is involved in the struggle. The men must triumph.

REID.

Triumph ! Then you really call into question the evidence of the books.

ELLEN.

This tale has been disproved a hundred times. All that concerns capital is false and corrupt. Capital must be destroyed.

LADY ANNE.

Of course, Miss Sands; but may I ask if it was only that I might hear your views on this all-absorbing question that you forced your way into my house ?

ELLEN.

No, Lady Anne, it was not. Matters have

arrived at a crisis, and we do not know on what side—can I still say our leader, is fighting.

LADY ANNE.

Indeed.   It seems to me that Mr. Reid has very clearly defined his position.

ELLEN.

Have you gone over to the other side?

REID.

If to state the truth is to go over to the other side, I have done so.

LADY ANNE.

Are you satisfied, Miss Sands?

ELLEN.

I fully understand! I do not contest Mr. Reid's right to change his opinions, but before every dissolution of partnership there is a general settling. There are certain matters on which I must speak to Mr. Reid alone.

LADY ANNE.

Miss Sands, you're presuming on the tolerance I extend to you—let me remind you that there are limits.   But perhaps this is a matter that Mr. Reid will settle for himself.

REID (*to* LADY ANNE).

I cannot refuse to discuss whatever matters Miss Sands may desire to discuss with me. You'll excuse me, Lady Anne. (LADY ANNE *bows coldly.*) Ellen, I'm at your service. (*To* LADY ANNE.)   It is not possible for me to do otherwise.   I'll return in a few minutes. (ELLEN *has moved towards the door.*)

LADY ANNE.

But, Miss Sands, there's no reason why you should leave.   You can talk with Mr. Reid here.   (*Gathers up the wool-work, and exit.*)

REID.

Ellen, we're alone. . . . You've come to speak to me on an important matter.

ELLEN.

Yes; and I'll not linger in the purely personal matter of the transference of your affections to Lady Anne, though that too must be settled. You've ceased to love me?

REID.

I'll waste no time in excuses.

ELLEN.

That's right—the mere fact.

REID.

I have.

ELLEN.

Ah, you love her, and will never care for me again. (*She sits down, buries her face in her hands, struggling with her emotion.*) An overmastering passion, the plea of every libertine. Oh, that you should have lied to me so—the utter vileness of it.

REID.

I didn't lie to you. When I told you last

10

week that I loved you, and that you could trust me, I thought I was speaking the truth. I was mistaken.

ELLEN (*getting up*).

After all, you're under no obligation to love me ; we're free to choose, and I suppose to rectify our mistakes. It must be so, only— only——

REID.

I thought it was only for the sake of the cause that you cared for me.

ELLEN.

Did she say so ? There are as many ways of loving as of living. She loves as she lives. I love as I live. (*Dashes a tear aside.*) And for the sake of this new love you have abandoned not only me, but the cause itself ?

REID.

No. It was the desperate policy you've pursued in the present strike that destroyed my belief—a policy that has brought men and women and children to the verge of starvation,

that will probably end in riot, violence, murder
—a policy that if pursued will reduce the
world to a desert, and change civilised man
back to a barbarian.

ELLEN.

Even that were better than the present system
should endure.

REID.

It is those very opinions that have produced
a change in mine.

ELLEN.

Are you sure, John ?

REID.

We're sure of nothing.   It were vain to argue
about motives—human motive is inscrutable.
You've come on a matter of urgent business ?

ELLEN.

Yes, on the most urgent business.

REID.

Then why have you not spoken before ?

ELLEN.

I hesitated.

REID.

You hesitated.   You undecided!

ELLEN.

You're gravely concerned in it. . . . But I must tell you.   There's a rumour of a large sum of money having been sent to the strike fund.   The letter that contained the cheque was directed to you.   It has been suggested that you suppressed the cheque so that you might more easily persuade the miners to return to work.

REID.

Who's my accuser?   No matter; do you believe him?

ELLEN.

I cannot believe such a thing of you.

REID.

Then why do you ask?

ELLEN.

Because your life will be in danger if the rumour proceeds further.

REID.

A word from you'll quench it at once.

ELLEN.

Exactly; and it is for the authority to speak that I come here.   A word from me is sufficient, and that word shall be spoken if you say that the rumour is false.

REID.

I can ask no favour from you.   We're fighting on different sides.

ELLEN.

Deny it; for if you do not——

REID.

You'll have to denounce me——

ELLEN.

I shall have to say that you declined to deny it, which amounts to the same thing.

REID.

And you'll do this?

ELLEN.

I must.

REID.

Then—Ellen——

ELLEN.

Hush; the time has passed for denial. A moment ago I should have taken your word. . . . Now I cannot. And so for her vicious sake you detained money that was sent to save men and women and children from famine.

REID.

It was for their sake I detained it. Is it worse to suppress a cheque that you know must lead to utter destruction than it is to tell men that books have been kept falsely and urge them to persevere in a mad endeavour which you know must end in their ruin?

ELLEN.

Which I know!

REID.

Which the slightest exercise of common sense must tell you will lead them into irretrievable disaster; and you did this for the sake of theories which, when put to the test, may prove as vain as the wind. You lied to them for the sake of your theories—I held my tongue for their welfare; which of us is the greater culprit?

ELLEN.

I do not believe those books; in the way of man's regeneration there are many pitfalls.

REID.

There are indeed, and I'm not the only one.

ELLEN.

We've not come together to discuss, but to

act. Immediately your treachery is known your life will be forfeited—you must fly the town.

REID.

They shall listen to me, I will save them. Justice and good sense shall triumph. I'll go to them whom you say are waiting to assassinate me, and in the market-place I'll confute you and your friends, who would lead them on to their ruin.

ELLEN.

Do not go to the market-place if you value your life.

REID.

If I carry the men with me my life will become of value; if I fail, I may as well perish at their hands as any other way.

ELLEN.

I shall not help you—you go at your peril.

REID.

I do not ask your help. (*Exit.*)

ELLEN (*speaking like one in a dream*).

He's gone to his death. I cannot save him.
He detained the money for her sake.

(*She turns and goes out slowly. The* FOOT-
MAN *enters a moment after with a
lamp. He places it on the table, looks to
the wicks, draws curtains, goes back to
lamp. A minute and a half elapses; then
a knocking is heard at window opening on
to lawn.*)

FOOTMAN.

Who is there?

STEINBACH.

Baron Steinbach; open at once. (*The* FOOT-
MAN *opens window. Enter* STEINBACH *dressed
in a long travelling overcoat.*) Where's her ladyship?

FOOTMAN.

I think her ladyship is in her room.

STEINBACH.

Then send to her, and say that I'm waiting to speak to her on a matter that does not admit of delay. (*Enter* LADY ANNE.) Oh, here is Lady Anne. (FOOTMAN *withdraws.*) I was just sending the footman to you with a message that you were to come to me at once.

LADY ANNE.

What is it? What has happened?

STEINBACH.

The town is mad with famine, the men's leaders are losing all control, wild threats are being uttered, and at this moment a riotous feeling may begin. I've telegraphed for a detachment of soldiers; it is doubtless on its way here. In the meantime, in the meantime—— (*Looks at his watch.*) It will not arrive for at least two hours yet.

LADY ANNE.

But he? Where is he? Where are they?

STEINBACH.

Who?

LADY ANNE.

John Reid and Ellen Sands; they were here a short time ago. Have they gone?

STEINBACH.

Reid passed me at the bottom of the garden. He was calling to the people. Crowds followed him. I asked a passer-by what was the meaning of it. He said Reid was on his way to the market-place to address a meeting.

LADY ANNE.

So she's succeeded in persuading him; she's won him over, and he's gone to betray me.

STEINBACH.

Gone to betray you! What do you mean, Anne?

LADY ANNE.

I'd better tell you all. When John Reid came here last week to examine the books; when he left the library convinced that the men's demands were impracticable, Ellen Sands arrived with a letter ; that letter contained a cheque for £2000.

STEINBACH.

And for your sake he suppressed the fact of the arrival of the cheque, intending to acknowledge it when he had persuaded the abandonment of the strike and the men were once more safely in the mine.

LADY ANNE.

It was not for my sake, but for theirs that he suppressed the cheque.

STEINBACH.

A specious sophistry, but one which not even he would have accepted had it not received the endorsement of your love.

LADY ANNE.

You wrong us both.

STEINBACH.

It may be as you say.   Events have, however,

proved too strong for him.   So that was the
way you tried to arrange things?   My dear, my
dear Anne, you had much better have confided
in me.   My advice alone will prove valid.

LADY ANNE.

So this man has gone.

STEINBACH.

To be torn to pieces in the market-place.

LADY ANNE.

They may listen to him ; he may carry them
with him.

STEINBACH.

He can only have gone there to explain the
excellence of his intentions.

LADY ANNE.

You do not believe——

STEINBACH.

It matters not what I believe, but if he con-
fesses that he detained that cheque his life isn't

worth three minutes' purchase. . . . To think that a man should be such a fool—vanity—belief in his eloquence. . . . Ah! what's that? Crowds still going to the market-place. We shall be able to watch the effect of his oratory from this window. (*Draws the curtain.*)

LADY ANNE.

Not at this hour.

STEINBACH.

The moon is up. (*Throwing open the window.*) The market-place is as bright as the day. All the town seems to be there. I think they have let him get on the platform; but it is difficult to distinguish detail. . . . Have you a pair of opera-glasses?

LADY ANNE (*snatching a pair from the table*).

Yes, there's one. Is he on the platform?

STEINBACH.

Yes, I think so.

LADY ANNE.

Do they listen?

STEINBACH (*altering the glasses*).

The light is deceitful, and these glasses are
not very suited to my sight.

LADY ANNE (*snatching the glasses from him*).

Then give them to me.

STEINBACH (*coming down stage*).

Can you see?

LADY ANNE.

Yes, perfectly.

(STEINBACH *sits in arm-chair.*)

STEINBACH.

Your friend doesn't seem to be wanting in
courage. It requires no small pluck to face a
mob like that . . . and with such a tale. How
can he hope? Imagination, courage, but no
brains. . . . Do they listen?

LADY ANNE.

I do not know . . . tell me, will they kill him? Yes, they are listening to him. (*Turning from the window.*)

STEINBACH.

I'm glad of it. I've no reason to wish him well, but such a death!

LADY ANNE (*turning to the window*).

But now there is a movement amongst the crowd; it seems to threaten him.

STEINBACH.

Then he's doomed. The first blow's struck, and nothing can save him.

LADY ANNE.

They crowd round the platform! Can we do nothing to save him?

STEINBACH.

I see that you're still in love with him.

LADY ANNE.

You needn't be in love with a man because

you don't wish to see him torn to pieces under your very eyes. They have not struck him yet. But why does he remain? Ah, he's fighting now. But he overpowers the brute, and has thrown him from his platform.

STEINBACH.

There's plenty more behind that ruffian. Once they're blooded they'll have at him and tear him like hounds a hare.

LADY ANNE.

He's retreated; they've driven him into a corner.

(STEINBACH *gets up and takes* LADY ANNE *from the window.*)

STEINBACH.

Anne, this is no sight for you ; come away.

LADY ANNE.

See if they've killed him. Here, take the glasses.

STEINBACH.

You saw them drive him into a corner of

11

the square, whence there is no egress. It is
vain to think further about him.

LADY ANNE.

I do not speak so cruelly, and he went
there to betray me.

STEINBACH.

I did not mean to be cruel. What a death,
what a reward for his labours ! He gave up
everything for them.

LADY ANNE.

Yes, everything. This is shocking. Oh, that
I ever came here !

STEINBACH.

You're trembling. . . . This has unnerved
you. We must go away at once.

LADY ANNE.

Take me away.

STEINBACH.

We must escape at once.

LADY ANNE.

Escape !

STEINBACH.

At the railway station we shall be safe.   My
yacht is at Southampton.   My villa on the
Italian coast is at your service should you
not care to remain in England.

LADY ANNE.

To leave here defeated, scouted the reputed
mistress of a socialist.

STEINBACH.

My dear Anne, we should never show our
hearts, nor any volatile fragment of our hearts,
outside of our own society.

LADY ANNE.

Oh ! this is disgraceful.   It was cruel of him
to betray me.

STEINBACH.

He sacrificed you to his honour, and we've
seen how the populace appreciated the sacrifice.
Come, Anne, come . . . go for a wrap, and let's
get away at once.

LADY ANNE.

Flight !

STEINBACH.

You shall be revenged. To-morrow the mine
will be under military protection. Non-unionist
labour shall be imported, cost what it may, and
you shall dictate your own terms. Now go for
a wrap, and let us go away at once.

> (*Exit* LADY ANNE, *right.* STEINBACH
> *looks at his watch. He goes to the
> window.*)

Crowds coming this way. . . . If that fellow
should have escaped, he'll be sure to come after
her. . . . Then we shall have the town down
upon us; the house will be pillaged. (*Returning,
left.*) Anne, Anne, I beg you to hasten.

> (*Enter* LADY ANNE, *wrapped in shawl.*)

LADY ANNE.

I'm ready. Come, let's lose no time. A
multitude seems to fill the street. . . . I'm
frightened. If you weren't here what should
I do ?

STEINBACH.

You treated me shockingly, but I was determined to win you.

> (*They go towards the window that leads on to the lawn. Enter* REID, *torn and haggard.*)

Have no fear. In a week we shall be in Italy.

REID.

So you are going away with him?

> (LADY ANNE *and* STEINBACH *turn round.*)

LADY ANNE.

You escaped the mob, then?

REID.

I escaped the mob.

LADY ANNE.

Are you hurt?

REID.

Mortally, though hardly a blow reached me.

LADY ANNE.

We were watching from that window, and we thought that we saw you killed.

REID.

I escaped by a miracle. A door was suddenly opened—I fled through it; it was closed behind me—I know not by whom. I fled through the house, climbed some walls, dodged the crowd through some back streets. . . . I've come back to find you leaving with Baron Steinbach.

LADY ANNE.

Why did you betray me?

REID.

Did I betray any one but myself?

LADY ANNE.

And after betrayal and broken promises you returned here expecting——

REID.

Forgive my poor expectations—they are my

last. So you are going away with Baron Steinbach?

LADY ANNE.

I am flying for my life. . . . If Baron Steinbach were not here——

REID.

You could not look to me for help? Truly you could not.

LADY ANNE.

You cannot remain here. You'll be taken and torn to pieces. You must escape.

STEINBACH (*coming down the stage*).

Lady Anne is right, you must escape; it is too horrible.

REID.

Spare me your pity, Baron Steinbach. Spare me that. You've won on every side. Be satisfied with your victory.

STEINBACH.

You misunderstand me. I intended no insult.

Let our former antagonism be forgotten.   Let
me help you——

REID.

I do not need your help or any one's.   I'm
no coward, and will meet my fate as it should
be met.

STEINBACH.

We do not doubt your courage, but it cannot
avail you against numbers.   If you leave this
house you'll be killed.   But you're safe here,
and at daybreak you can escape.   I'll see that
help is sent, and afterwards—— (REID *looks at*
STEINBACH.   STEINBACH *turns from* REID *to*
LADY ANNE.)   Anne, we must go away.   (*He
looks once more at* REID.)

REID.

Think no more of me.   That is the greatest
kindness.

STEINBACH.

But you'll do what I say?   You'll remain
here till daybreak?

REID.

Yes, I'll remain here.

LADY ANNE.

And at daybreak you'll escape?

REID.

I shall escape.

STEINBACH.

Lady Anne, come away. (REID *sinks into a chair.*) Come, Lady Anne, come.

LADY ANNE (*from the window that opens on to lawn*).

Will he escape?

STEINBACH.

He says so. Come, I insist.

(*Exeunt* LADY ANNE *and* STEINBACH. REID *watches for a moment.*)

REID.

They have gone. They have gone away

together. (*Goes to window, left. Listens, and comes down the stage.*) There is no time to lose; they have discovered that I am here. (*Puts bottle on table.*)

(*Enter* ELLEN.)

ELLEN.

They've tracked you here. The house will soon be surrounded. You must escape at once.

REID.

And you came here to warn me?

ELLEN.

Yes.

REID.

Thank you.

ELLEN.

Escape, escape while there's yet time.

REID.

Escape. Why should I escape? For why?

ELLEN.

For her sake.

REID.

I escaped the mob only to find her leaving for Italy with Baron Steinbach.

ELLEN.

So she deceived you.

REID.

No, I am the deception, the only deception, and that deception is about to cease.

ELLEN.

You mean suicide?

REID.

Yes, escapement from self. I put it to you— you're a sensible girl, Ellen, and you don't lie. You'll not deceive me. Remember that you once loved me.

ELLEN.

Yes, I once loved you.

REID.

Thank you for those words. Now listen. I have lost all. I have betrayed the woman I loved, and I have been betrayed by her. I've betrayed the woman who loved me. I have lost not only her love but her respect. Worse than all, I've lost honour; never again can I look the world in the face. Belief in the cause is gone too—everything is gone—I stand a moral bankrupt. In such juncture of circumstances man must escape from self, I ask you is this not so?

ELLEN.

I cannot see that you could ever find happiness again in life, either for yourself or others.

REID.

That is how I feel, Ellen. I suppose all suicides feel the same. . . . It would have been better if I'd gone down fighting. . . . The brutes, I still feel their foul breaths on my face, and their foul hands. I abandoned my own class for their sake, but I never could assimilate my life with theirs. I'm not of any class or of any convictions. Why should I remain?

ELLEN.

No, no, you must not do this.

REID.

What would you have me do?

ELLEN.

Escape at once. . . . No, at daybreak.

REID.

Skulk out of the town at daybreak, and live face to face with my dishonour. Ellen, there is but one thing to be done.

(*A pause, during which* ELLEN *struggles with her emotion.*)

ELLEN.

It is very terrible, but I suppose it is as you say. (*Pause.*) Have you the means?

REID.

Yes. It appears that about a year ago her old favourite dog had to be poisoned. This remained.

ELLEN.

So the poison came from her. She's the world's poison. (*Pause.*) They're all about the house. They'll break in soon. . . . But they shall not kill you.

REID.

I'm safe from them. A moment and it is done. (*Pause.*) You'll forgive me the pain I've caused you. You'll forgive my want of faith. You'll forgive everything? You'll try to remember when my worst faults press hardest on your memory that I honestly desired the light, and that I sought although I did not find.

ELLEN.

All is forgiven to the dead.

REID.

Good-bye, Ellen. (*Kisses her on her forehead.*)

Good-bye. You must not remain here. (*He leads her to the door.*) Good-bye, Ellen. (*Exit.*) (*He looks at poison. He goes to the cabinet, gets some water, dissolves the strychnine, and comes down the stage, the glass in his hand, with his back partly turned to the audience; he raises the glass to drink; as he does so, the curtain falls.*)

CURTAIN.

THE WALTER SCOTT PRESS, NEWCASTLE-ON-TYNE.

Crown 8vo, Cloth, Price 6s.

A VOLUME OF ESSAYS BY GEORGE MOORE.

MODERN PAINTING.

Extract from a lengthy notice of this work by
Mr. WALTER PATER in the "Daily Chronicle"
of 10th June 1893.

"A lover of French art, in its various phases, the drift of Mr.
Moore's charge against contemporary English art, especially
under academic patronage, is that it is not vernacular; that the
degenerate sons of Reynolds and Constable are leaving their
native earth, and with it the roots and sources of their own
proper strength, actually for this very France of his own preference. Impressionism, to use that word, in the absence of any
fitter one,—the impressionism which makes his own writing on
art in this volume so effective, is, in short, the secret both of his
likes and dislikes, his hatred of what he thinks conventional and
mechanic, together with his very alert and careful evaluation of
what comes home to him as straightforward, whether in
Reynolds, or Rubens, or Ruysdael, in Japan, in Paris, or in
modern England; with Mr. Whistler, for instance, and Mr.
Sargent; his belief in the personal, the uncontrollable. Above
all that can be learnt in art, he would assure us—beyond all that
can be had of teachers—there is something there, something in
every veritable work of art, of the incommunicable, of what is
unique, and this is, perhaps, the one thing really of value in art.
As a personal quality or power it will vary greatly, in the case
of this or that work or workman, in its appeal to those who,
being outsiders in the matter of art, are nevertheless sensitive
and sincerely receptive, towards it. It will vary also, in a lesser
degree, even to those who in this matter *really know*. But to
the latter, at all events, preference in art will be nothing less
than conviction, and the estimate of artistic power and product,
in every several case, an object of no manner of doubt at all,
such as may well give a man, as in Mr. Moore's own case, the
courage of his opinions. In such matter opinion is, in fact, of
the nature of the sensations one cannot help."

London : WALTER SCOTT, LIMITED, 24 Warwick Lane.

www.ingramcontent.com/pod-product-compliance
Lightning Source LLC
Chambersburg PA
CBHW020226030726
47497CB00009B/2971